HEARTBREAK AT ROOSEVELT RANCH

ROOSEVELT RANCH BOOK 2

ELISE FABER

HEARTBREAK AT ROOSEVELT RANCH
Copyright © 2018 ELISE FABER

Newsletter sign-up

HEARTBREAK AT ROOSEVELT RANCH
Copyright © 2018 ELISE FABER
Paperback ISBN-13: 978-1-946140-06-7
Ebook ISBN- 978-1-946140-02-9
Cover Art by Jena Brignola

ROOSEVELT RANCH SERIES

Disaster at Roosevelt Ranch

Heartbreak at Roosevelt Ranch

Collision at Roosevelt Ranch

Regret at Roosevelt Ranch

Desire at Roosevelt Ranch

To all the rough patches and how they make us stronger.
And for Sara. I love you and thank you so much for everything.

I straightened from putting the last plate into the dishwasher and stretched for a towel to wipe my hands. I was exhausted after twenty-four straight hours with the kids, and Rob still wasn't home. Not to mention, I needed to make cupcakes for Max's school—and somehow do it without sugar.

So the ensuing crash upstairs was not welcome.

Dropping the towel, I whisper-sprinted up to the second floor —running on tiptoes while hopping, leaping, and skipping over every toy obstacle, creaky floorboard, and rogue crayon along the way.

The light was on in Max's room, and considering that I had made this trek a half dozen times in the last hour, I was out of patience.

"You need to go to sleep," I growled, throwing open the door, my fierce mom glare already in place.

Except the devil child *was* asleep.

He'd fallen out of bed, crashed onto an entire village of Legos —scattering them to hell and back—and was dead asleep.

My heart gave a little squeeze even as the logical part of me recognized the giant mess I'd be picking up tomorrow.

It was just that face.

A cupid's bow of bright pink lips, slightly parted, rosy cheeks, and mussed hair. The boy was cute, and it was hard to believe he was part of me, that he'd come from my body.

I clucked my tongue at myself, knowing I was being ridiculous and romantic and *Melissa-like* because I'd spent the day with Kelly and her toddler, Abby.

My baby sister had a baby. And a man. And was all grown up—

Oh God. There I went with the tears again.

Swiping a finger under each eye, I navigated the minefield of toys as I made my way over to Max. I gave an internal grunt as I lifted the little—or not so little, anymore—monkey and tucked him back into bed.

One hastily constructed barrier of pillows and blankets and stuffed Minecraft toys later, and I was heading back out of the room.

I flicked the light off, started to leave—

"Too dark, Mommy," he murmured.

A sigh. Back on it went. "Good night, sweetheart."

"Night."

This time I made it to the top of the stairs before a sound stopped me.

It wasn't the kids. No. This was more like . . . buzzing?

I cocked my head and listened, then made my way to my bedroom, a growing pile of toys in my arms as I went.

The door was open, and I walked inside, dumping the pile on the coverlet before stopping to pinpoint the sound.

I felt my pockets for my cell. Not even two days before, I'd scoured the house for my phone, it somehow having fallen out of my pocket, ending up under the dresser. It had taken darn near fifty calls and a search of the entire house before I'd found it.

Those locating apps were all well and good, but they couldn't tell a person which room in a house their phone was. Which meant the app, for my day-to-day exploits, was pretty much useless.

I hardly left home at all except for the kids' activities and school pickup or drop off.

Or if Rob needed something down at the station.

And that was fine. My place was at home. The kids needed me, Rob needed me. It was just that sometimes . . .

No. Don't get sidetracked.

My phone *was* in my pocket. The sound wasn't coming from beneath the dresser.

It was coming from the bed.

I peered under, saw nothing, and I was reaching for Rob's flashlight in his nightstand when I realized where exactly the noise was originating from.

My hand slid between the mattress and box spring, jumping a little when the object buzzed against my fingers.

"What—?" I pulled it out, saw it was an older-looking iPhone. Why was there—

Then I saw the texts. An entire screen worth of them.

And my heart froze solid.

I'm heading to the hotel.

Where are you?

Don't keep me waiting, honey.

I need you.

The question wasn't why Rob had hidden a phone under his side of the mattress. It was why someone named Celeste was calling him honey and telling *my* husband that she needed him.

Downstairs, I heard the garage door rumble open and close, the clink of Rob's keys on the kitchen counter. "Miss?" he called softly up the stairs.

My voice was gone, my throat tight. My eyes burned, and still,

I held the phone. It wasn't until I heard him walking down the hall to the bedroom that I sprang into motion.

I shoved the phone back under the mattress and scooped up the toys.

Rob stopped short in the doorway. "Oh." He smiled. "I called you."

"Sorry, I was cleaning."

He touched my cheek, slid past me. "You don't have to do that."

"It's my job," I said brightly, and if it was too bright then what did it matter anyway?

My husband was moving toward the bathroom, already unbuttoning his shirt. "Is there a plate for me?"

I turned, saw he'd paused, and forced a smile. "Yup. I'll heat it up for you."

"Thanks, love."

"Of course." I walked out of the bedroom but didn't go downstairs.

Instead, I hesitated in the hall, silent and waiting.

And my gut tied itself into knots when I heard Rob's footfalls across the carpet, the slide of his hand beneath the mattress as he pulled out the phone.

2

"*M*OOOOOOOOM!"

The camera in my hands jumped, and that perfect angle, the *perfect* highlight of the sun's rays coming through my kitchen window and traipsing across my gorgeous display of a salad—if I did say so myself—disappeared in a flash.

No pun intended.

Footsteps pounded across the floor overhead. *Eight* feet. From two kids and one dog. The trio was streaking across the hallway, preparing to hurtle themselves down the stairs.

Which meant I had approximately twelve seconds to get the shot before chaos descended.

Back up on my tiptoes, extending my arm precariously over the plate as I leaned—read: contorted—myself in such a way as to obtain that perfect angle without marring the photograph with something as egregious as my shadow.

Bang. Bang. Bang.

"Ow!" Allie. She'd just turned five and was a terror on two legs. "I'm telling Mom!"

"Almost there," I puffed.

"It was *your* fault." Max. My sweet boy. Now eight and not so little.

"Ruff!" The dog. The terror on *four* legs. Rocco was seven months old and sixty pounds of exuberant energy, potty accidents, and counter surfing.

But Rob loved the fluffball.

Rob.

My eyes burned.

The trio slid around the corner into the kitchen, Rocco colliding with the far wall.

His brakes weren't great yet.

With the group's appearance, the noise level in the room rose to deafening.

Click.

I checked the shot and breathed out a sigh of relief. Perfect.

Stepping down from the stool I'd been perched on, I stashed my camera carefully out of reach of canine and human troublemakers then stowed the plate in the fridge. Another taste test wouldn't hurt, just to perfect the recipe.

And really, I wasn't going to waste one crumb of that goat cheese. Not when it was so expensive and difficult to find in Nowhere, Utah.

Or rather, Darlington, Utah.

"*Mom.*"

Max stood with his arms crossed. He was tall for his age with dark hair and eyes and the spitting image of Rob, a fact that made my bruised heart ache all the more.

Allie was like me: slender, tall, and blond with pale brown eyes and skin that never failed to burn in the sun.

We needed to invest in sunscreen stock. God knew we bought enough of the stuff.

Both kids were talking over each other, furious frowns pulling their brows down as they tried to prove their point . . . or, rather, ruin my eardrums by being the loudest.

Even Rocco chimed in with several well-timed barks.

I did what I always did in these situations.

I stood silently. And waited.

It never took long, I'd found. If I tried to raise my voice over theirs, tried to shout my way for quiet, like Rob did, nothing. He used his magical cop skills to reign tough over the kids—and dog, I thought, as Rocco eyed the countertop like it held a king's trove of treasure.

My voice didn't do that.

My glare did, however.

Rocco paused mid-leap and plunked his front paws back on the tile floor.

Max was the first human to stop contributing to the noise. Older and wiser, he was.

Allie went on for a few more beats before her eyes widened and her mouth clamped closed.

"Max, explain your side first."

"I was playing with my Legos, and Allie barged in and broke my set—"

"I did *not*!" Allie protested.

"It's not your turn to speak," I told her.

She huffed and crossed her arms.

"She broke my house, and I'll never be able to find all of the pieces, and I-I—" Tears welled in his brown eyes, and I had to steel my heart against those glistening orbs. He might be cute, but he was also smart.

Too smart for *my* good.

"Okay," I said. "Allie, your side."

"He took *my* Lego set, and I wanted to get the pieces back. It was my house, and he can't keep it."

"You let me borrow it!" Max said, indignant.

"I *want* it back."

"I—"

"You—"

I waited.

The second round took less time.

"What happens when you fight over toys?" I asked.

Two sets of eyes went wide. Rocco whined and lay down on the floor, burying his nose in his paws.

Max glanced at Allie. "How about you use my Legos and build your own house?"

Allie considered this. "And then when we're done we can switch back!"

Max nodded. "Okay."

They ran off, Rocco trailing their progress, leaving with as much noise as they'd entered the room.

"Ten minutes until bath time!" I called, but they were already out of earshot.

With a rueful smile, I pulled my plate from the fridge and a fork out of the drawer.

"You're sexy when you pull that stern glare out."

I shivered at the voice in my ear, the chest very close to my spine. My body knew my husband's on an intrinsic level, and so I didn't jump in surprise or shriek in fear.

Instead, I melted into his warmth, soaked up his scent.

"Hi, baby," he said with a soft kiss to the side of my neck.

"Hi, yourself." I turned, slipping carefully out of his embrace. Because even though I loved this man with every fiber of my being, he might not feel the same.

Text messages from another woman.

A hidden cell phone.

Sudden long hours away from his family.

Cheating.

There was a strong possibility that the man I loved was cheating on me.

---

3

*T*he snoring was killing me.

Absolutely killing me.

I rolled to my side, plunked my pillow over my head, and . . . it did absolutely nothing to muffle the sound of chainsaws erupting from my husband's nose and mouth.

"Rob," I said and poked him. "Roll over."

"Sorry," he muttered as he turned to the other side and promptly fell right back asleep. The snoring stopped, but the breathing didn't.

The heavy and very *loud* breathing.

I blew out a sigh and stared at the darkened ceiling. I don't know why I bothered. It was the same thing every time. He snored; I woke up. He stopped and went back to sleep. I stayed awake.

It was mom brain. The moment I was even partially awake, my mind raced and I started listing all of the things I needed to do for the next day.

I forgot to pack a snack for Max tomorrow.

Allie needs to wear orange, not the purple shirt I'd set out for her.

Rocco needs to go to the vet for his last set of shots.

A new blog post had to be created, new recipes tested, photos taken. All while the kids were in school. And to complicate things, Allie was in kindergarten, which was only half a day, so I got to add two trips—there and back—to school because neither of their pickup or drop off schedules aligned. So my four free hours were really only three, and now we had a dog who needed to be walked as well.

I closed my eyes, my chest tightening, my respirations shallow.

I'd spent so much of the last few months feeling overwhelmed. And for a girl like me—a tightly strung perfectionist who struggled to cut loose—that was almost the kiss of death.

Unstrapped from a roller coaster that raced along the tracks, barely hanging on by my fingertips.

My eyes flashed open. There was no way I was going back to sleep now.

Carefully, I slid from beneath the comforter and slipped from the bed. Rocco wagged his tail in his crate, a little rap that had me shushing him as I navigated the shadows. I closed the bathroom door behind me. Only then did I flip on the light.

Which wasn't kind. Thank you, fluorescents.

The woman I saw in the mirror wasn't quite a stranger, but she didn't look like me.

Not exactly anyway.

She was older. Plainer. *Grayer.*

Gross.

Look. I got it, I know we're all supposed to be kind to ourselves, to love our wrinkles and gray hairs, but dammit, four o'clock allowed for some self-pity.

Okay?

I released a sigh. Not okay.

The problem with being a perfectionist is that it carried over to all parts of my life. My skin didn't glow enough, my stomach wasn't as flat as it had once been, my ass wasn't high and tight, my thighs jiggled—

And now *that* was enough self-hate for this time of day.

I glared at my pale brown eyes in the mirror, warning the inner haters to shut it before splashing water on my face and pulling a brush through my hair. I scrubbed my teeth, slapped on some deodorant, and then made my way into the closet.

My favorite stretchy skinny jeans were fresh out of the wash, and I wrestled my way into them, pairing the dark denim with a blue floral blouse and a stack of necklaces.

I snagged a pair of flats but wouldn't put them on until I was well away from the Sleeping Beauties. A swipe of mascara and a quick application of blush were the final touches I added before I turned off the bathroom light and waited for my eyes to readjust to the dark.

Rob was back to snoring when I crept through the bedroom. I shook my head and closed the door behind me, heading for the top of the stairs.

That was when I heard the first noise.

A moan. The rustling of bedclothes. I dropped my shoes and bolted for Allie's bedroom.

She began crying.

"Mom!"

I skirted the mess of toys on the floor, picking my way across with all the finesse of an American Ninja Warrior.

"What's wrong, honey?" I asked.

"I don't—"

I was already reaching for her when she exploded.

Okay, not exploded exactly. More like Poltergeist-vomited, all over me. It dripped down my hair, soaked into my blouse, my jeans, the carpet, and bedding.

Perfect. Just perfect.

Allie began crying in earnest, and I soothed her as I swept her into my arms. We made it to the bathroom in record time.

I set her down in front of the toilet, holding her hair back when she gagged again and again. "I'm sorry, honey," I said when she stopped. Then I wet a towel and wiped her face and neck. "Let's get you out of these clothes."

She was shaking, tears sliding down her cheeks. "I'm sorry, Mommy."

"Shh. Not your fault." I wrapped her in a towel and cuddled her close until she stopped shivering. "Let's get you a quick bath, and then I'll set you up on the couch, okay?"

"O-okay."

Fifteen minutes later she was in clean pajamas, wrapped in blankets, and tucked into the couch, a bucket within arm's reach.

I went back upstairs to strip the sheets and clean the carpet. Then I carried all of the dirty linens back down to the laundry room and tossed them in the washer. By now the vomit had mostly dried on my clothes and hair, and I was in desperate need of a shower.

Time would tell if this was the stomach bug plague or if Allie had just eaten something that didn't agree with her.

Would one fall? Or would they all?

I snorted quietly as I slipped back into the bedroom, only to be bowled over by Rocco, wagging tail and wriggly butt. Rob must have let him out. He sniffed the carpet, did a one-eighty.

Uh-oh, potty time.

"Come on," I said, opening the door.

He pushed past me and sprinted down the stairs. I hustled after him, not wanting him to wake up Allie, who'd finally fallen back asleep.

But I needn't have worried. He bypassed the living room completely and went straight to the back door. "Good boy," I told him and opened it just wide enough for him to slip out. The icy morning breeze shot through the gap, having the dual effect of kicking up the smell of puke on my person and cutting directly through my still-damp clothes.

I shivered. "Hurry up, dog."

Rocco took a few more minutes. It was too cold to leave him outside, young as he was. Of course, *he* was the one with the thick fur.

Finally, he was done and sprinted for the opening into the house.

Or rather, crashed into the door, since those brakes were still under training.

"Come on, goofy," I told him as I snagged his collar and corralled him past the sleeping Allie on the sofa.

I'd already lost count of the trips up and down the stairs and it wasn't even six yet. Who said my butt wasn't high and tight? At this rate, I'd be a Kardashian in no time. Rocco wriggled his way alongside me, not fighting when I stuck him back in his kennel. Though that was probably because I promised him breakfast after I'd showered.

The bathroom light shone through the crack in the bottom of the door, and the bed was empty.

That plus the absence of chainsaw sounds told me Rob was in the bathroom.

Who was the detective now? I thought with a smirk.

I crossed to the bathroom and opened the door.

Or tried to.

It was locked.

I frowned.

Tried again.

"Rob?" I knocked, tilted my head when I heard . . . was he talking to someone? "Rob?" I asked louder.

The sounds inside the bathroom cut off. After a pause, he called, "Miss?"

"The door is locked."

Another pause. Then footsteps. The locked *clicked* before the door swung open. Rob was wrapped in a towel, his chest bare and glittering with drops of water. Normally, I'd have been distracted by those little beads of liquid. Today I barely noticed because there was a mark on his neck.

A suspicious bruise on the base of his throat—

Where someone might have kissed him.

And that someone had not been me.

Rob smiled, but it looked strained. "Sorry, hon. Force of habit." He turned and walked into the closet, closing the door behind him.

I was still on the threshold, blinking after him, when the door popped back open and he stuck his head out. "You look cute, by the way."

Before I could stammer out a thanks, the door shut again.

Had he not noticed the puke? Or was he trying to be nice because it looked like I'd been put through the wringer?

Or perhaps most important of all, had I imagined the mark?

4

---

*A*s with most moms, my shower was short and cold.
Between Allie's bath, the laundry, and Rob's shower, all the hot water was gone. Again.

Which didn't normally bother me, except I was coated in dried puke, had to wash my hair, and it was approximately minus eight thousand degrees outside.

Okay, fine. I exaggerated.

But still.

I rushed the shower, hissing as the cold water streamed from my hair and down my back.

Rob came out of the closet just as I stepped out, shivering more violently than Allie had been an hour earlier. He wore a button-down shirt, tie, and slacks.

"You look nice," I said, unable to ignore the fact that the shirt covered his neck. Should I pull it down and confront him?

"Meeting with the chief today."

Darlington was too small for its own police force. Rob worked at the county sheriff's office. The bigger force meant more resources for our little group of towns and better coverage.

"What about?" I asked as I wrapped a towel around my head.

"A case I've been working on."

"What case?" I ran the towel up one leg, then the other. Rob's eyes followed the movement.

"Can't talk about it yet," he said. I frowned, but before I could press his answer—we always discussed his cases, if not in specifics then at least in generals—he went on, "When was the last time you had something besides a salad?"

I straightened, pulling the towel around my breasts. "What do you mean?"

"You're too thin, Miss."

"What?"

He crossed over to me, pulling the towel open and splaying one hand over my side.

My heart skipped a beat. Calloused fingers. Rough skin against smooth. I forgot about the bruise on his neck, about the phone and suspicions. I wanted his hand to move.

Up or down. I almost didn't care.

I *needed* him to touch me.

His head dropped next to mine, hot breath on my neck, my ear. "You need to eat more."

It took a second for the words to process. I stiffened, leaned back.

Not that it mattered since Rob had already stepped away.

"This isn't like college," I said. "I am eating."

He studied me for a long moment, dark eyes piercing, black hair slightly damp and hanging over his forehead.

I wanted to push the strands back, like I used to.

Instead, my throat tightened when he tugged the sides of my towel together, tucking the cotton sheet under each arm.

"Keep it that way," he said.

"I like salads." My tone was defensive, but then again so was his.

"Add some protein to them."

Eyes burning, I turned away. "Check on Allie before you leave, she woke up puking but is back asleep on the couch. I'll be down in a bit."

I walked into the closet and closed the door, leaned back against it.

We used to leave doors open, no barriers between us.

And now . . .

I was glad the wood was there.

———

THE HOUSE WAS quiet when I made my way downstairs, hair in a ponytail, jeans and blouse swapped for sweats and a T-shirt.

If Max was next on the plague patrol, I wanted to be prepared.

Rocco's crate had been empty when I'd gotten out of the bathroom, so I hustled to the back door, in case Rob had taken him outside to go potty and forgotten to let him back in.

I flicked on the floodlights and saw the yard was empty.

Hmm.

The pup was usually great about staying nearby and out of trouble. He didn't go to the bathroom in the house—at least not too often anymore—and there wasn't any food out for him to snag off the counter. He also didn't chew anything except shoes, and we'd taken to keeping those in our closets so—

My flats. I'd left them at the top of the stairs when I'd gone to Allie. I ran up the steps and groaned.

One was missing.

It was always the left shoe.

I snagged the right one and ran back to the kitchen. No Rocco. He wasn't in the laundry or dining rooms either.

Which meant.

I walked into the living room and saw him, curled up like the cute demon he was, right at Allie's feet. Gnawing. On. My. Shoe.

When there were a half dozen chew toys scattered across the carpet.

I dropped my head back to look at the ceiling, counted to five, and snagged a rubber bone from the floor. His ears dropped when I approached, the sad, poor little puppy dog eyes in full force.

"I'm not letting you keep it," I muttered. "I don't care if it's ruined."

He whined and dropped his head to what had once been half of my favorite pair of flats. Brushed gray suede with turquoise bows.

"This," I said, and swapped it for the bone, "is your chew toy. Not my shoes."

Rocco whined again and gave me a pathetic look.

"I still love you."

His tailed tapped against the couch.

"A little."

He grumbled but buried his nose into the blankets and closed his eyes.

Shaking my head, I went into the kitchen and tossed the shoes in the trash. Then I called the sick line for school, leaving a message saying Allie would be out that day.

I moved the laundry around, pulled out my notebook of recipes, and had just opened my laptop when I heard a noise that made my gut churn.

Retching.

I ran into the living room, but Allie was still asleep.

Another trip up the stairs—*this* is why I was thin, freaking two-story houses—and found Max bent over the toilet.

I rubbed his back, gave him a cool cloth, and sat next to him.

He glanced up at me with bloodshot eyes. "I didn't make it, Mom," he said. "I'm sorry."

"In bed?"

A nod. "And the carpet."

I closed my eyes. Not even six-thirty and I was exhausted.

"I'm sorry," he said and his chin wobbled.

"Not your fault, buddy," I told him. "I'm sorry you're not feeling well." I handed him a cup of water to swish his mouth. Luckily he hadn't gotten puke on his clothes, since there wasn't any hot water. "Can you wait for a bath?"

He nodded.

"Okay. Let's get you settled downstairs."

"Can you carry me?"

This is why I was thin, Rob, I thought as I carried sixty pounds of kid down to the living room, before running back up to fetch blankets and a pillow. *Then* repeating the trip to bring the dirties to the laundry room and switch everything around.

I'd barely managed to get Max's carpet cleaned when I felt the swirling in my gut.

Oh God. I'd known I would fall eventually. I'd just hoped—

For what exactly? To be spared? For a miracle?

Those didn't happen to me. Not any longer, at any rate.

Moisture pooled in my mouth, my stomach rumbled. Dropping the cloth I was holding, I sprinted to the bathroom and barely made it to the toilet before I heaved.

The plague was upon me.

*R*ob shrugged off his suit jacket the moment he walked into his office. His promotion to detective had been a great opportunity, something that he'd wanted for years.

Unfortunately, it came with the suit requirement.

He loosened his tie, undid the top button of his shirt, and logged into his computer.

Just after seven in the morning, the precinct was fairly quiet.

Which was just the way he liked it.

Fewer people, fewer distractions, a smaller risk of getting caught.

"Fuck," he muttered, grabbing the mouse and pulling up his email. He was waiting to hear back on a set of prints that had been discovered at a meth lab in Campbell, the next town over from Darlington.

Campbell, Darlington, and Douglasville formed the Tri-Hills community. Separate they were too small to each house decent fire and police departments. Together meant they had more resources and could afford better equipment and staffing.

But that also meant that he was dealing with crimes that Darlington itself didn't often experience.

Drugs were nearly nonexistent in his hometown. However,

Campbell was more isolated and closer to the border of Colorado —which had legalized marijuana.

Consequently there was some spillover into their small Utah community.

Not that meth and pot were on the same level, but they had seen a rise in seemingly drug-related crimes—burglary, muggings, home invasions—in recent months.

Which meant there was a new player in town.

His job was to figure out how to take that person, or people, down.

Simple, that, he thought with a sigh. *If only it were easier than clearing his inbox.*

Rob had one hundred and sixty unread emails, all sent overnight, but none of them was the one he'd logged in to see.

He wanted answers, dammit. Especially since he'd seen those fingerprints with his own eyes . . . or the bruises created by their owner, anyway.

Angry purple marks marring the skin of a young girl who'd stared sightlessly up at the ceiling. Her skirt hiked up, her shirt torn, blood trickling from the corner of her mouth.

But it had been her bracelet that made him remember her. That made the case personal.

Strings of yarn woven together, knots sloppily tied.

He didn't know if a younger sibling had made it for her or a babysitting charge or if it was something totally different.

The trouble was that he couldn't get his own kids out of his mind.

He pictured Max, tongue poking out as he concentrated, carefully knotting yarn together. He imagined Allie picking colors— pink, pink, and more pink—to make a bracelet for Callie, their babysitter.

And then his mind swapped Callie for the girl in the house.

Rob blew out a breath and shoved up from his desk, his chair teetering then colliding against the wall with a *bang.*

"Hey."

The voice was soft, feminine, and sexy as hell.

Which meant he knew exactly who it was before he even glanced up from straightening the chair.

"Celeste," he murmured.

A flash of white teeth framed in lush fire engine red. Curves for days encased in the department's blues. Blond hair pulled into a perky ponytail.

Breasts. Ass. Hips. Waist.

This woman had it all.

Just not for him. He preferred his women thin and lithe, like his wife.

She closed the door, thrust out her breasts as she leaned back against it. "I need you."

"I'm busy," he said.

"Too busy for me?" Celeste pursed her lips in a pout.

"Yes."

She laughed.

Because apparently she liked a challenge.

Or wouldn't take no for an answer.

She strode forward like a model traversing a catwalk, all smoldering eyes and swaying hips.

Shit. Here they went. Again.

The chair slipped from his grip and bumped into his desk. The little frame standing next to his monitor rattled, fell forward.

His family's smiling faces disappeared.

Celeste crossed around his desk, drew his hands to her waist, and . . . rose on tiptoe.

He fended off her octopus arms then pushed her backward until the ass that the rest of the department drooled over was firmly seated in the chair in front of his desk.

"Spill it, Celeste."

She smiled and it was wide and predatory. "Want to hear about the case we're working together?"

Fuck. His. Life.

"I'm dying," I told Kelly into the phone.

"I'll come over," my sister said immediately. "Abby and I will distract the kids so you can get a break."

"No," I said. "We're on quarantine. Stomach bug. I don't want Abby to get sick."

"Oh no!" Kel said. "The kids picked up something from school?"

"Yup," I said. "And then me."

My sister groaned. "That sucks." A pause. "Anything I can do? I can pick stuff up from the store and leave it on the porch, prison style."

I shook my head but promptly stopped when it made a wave of dizziness blur my vision. "How is that prison style?" I asked, flopping back onto the couch cushions.

"I don't know—" A cry echoed through the airwaves. "Oh, that's Abby."

"Mom," Allie whined, suddenly appearing like whack-a-mole next to the couch arm. "I'm hungry."

I put one finger up, indicating that Allie needed to wait. "I think both of our kids are saying the same thing, albeit in different ways," I told my sister. "Thanks for the offer. I'll see you soon."

"Call me if you need anything—" Another angry cry interrupted her. "Love you. Bye!"

I hung up and closed my eyes for a moment, trying to summon the energy to move. The problem with being the last to get sick was that the first person to fall was usually recovered by then, and if patient zero was a kid . . .

Recovery time was seriously limited.

"Mooom!" Allie said. "I'm so, so, so, so, *so* hungry."

My lips twitched, and I opened my eyes. "Let's see what I can do about that, okay?"

We walked into the kitchen together, and I pulled a bottled sports drink out of the fridge, then some saltines from the pantry. I poured her a small glass and put a handful of crackers on a napkin.

"Start with this. You hold it down, and I'll make you something else, okay?"

"Okay," she said, spraying the table with a fine mist of cracker crumbs and spit, since she'd already gobbled down several of the bland squares.

I sank down in the chair opposite her, the sleeve of crackers in my hand. My stomach was not ready for anything, not even the cardboard-like snack.

Allie didn't seem to mind the taste, however. She pounded down the little meal and asked for more.

"Let's watch one episode of *Bubble Guppies*, and if you don't throw up then I'll make you dinner, okay?"

Brown eyes fixed me in place. "Mac and cheese," she said. "From the blue box."

I shuddered. It was a favorite of kids everywhere. Pasta and fake, powdery cheese that tasted like socks.

It was also probably the single meal that I had enough energy to make at that point in time.

"Deal," I said.

"Woohoo!" Allie streaked from the kitchen and launched herself onto the couch. "*Bubble Guppies* and mac and cheese!"

Max glanced up from his iPad—yes, they both had an iPad and don't judge, I'd bought them on sale last Black Friday. But they had literally paid for themselves that afternoon alone. "*Bubble Guppies* is stupid."

"Is not!"

"Is too."

Distraction was key when a parent was sick and alone.

"Max, pick a new app to download," I interrupted. "Allie, what episode?"

And with Rob working long hours—

"Really?" Max said. "I can?"

"I want the parade one," Allie said and danced around. "I love *Bubble Guppies*!"

"Pick one from your wish list," I told him, not wanting him to spend the entire episode deciding. "Allie, it's starting," I said after deftly scrolling through the On Demand program and choosing the correct episode.

"How about this one?"

I glanced at the price—$4.99—and grimaced. I hated paying for apps, let alone that much. Still, I really wanted twenty-three minutes of peace and quiet.

And so I caved.

Ten seconds later, it was downloading and I was closing my eyes on the couch.

"Mom! It's over!"

My eyes flew open. Why were my kids always shouting?

"Want to watch another one?" I asked, voice gravelly as I struggled to sit up.

"No," she said. "I'm hungry!"

My sigh was pathetic. I knew it was. It still didn't have any effect on my kids.

"I'm hungry too," Max announced.

"You still have to pass the puke test." I shoved myself up from the couch.

He giggled. "You said puke."

"Yup." I smiled and smacked a kiss on top of his head. "We've had a lot of puke all over the place today."

Wiry arms wrapped around my middle. "I love you, Mommy."

And my heart melted. "Come on," I said, hugging him back. "Let's go cook up some cardboard."

————

THE BED DIPPED, and I rolled over to see Rob sitting on the side of the bed.

"Is there anything for dinner?" he asked.

"Not today," I said. "We were all sick."

His dark brows pulled down. "You were? Why didn't you call me?"

"I texted you three times."

"You did? I didn't get them." He pulled out his cell and unlocked it. The little green box had a red bubble with a three in the upper right corner. He tapped it and, lo and behold, my messages were there.

Any chance you can come home early? The stomach plague has hit.

I'm feeling really lousy, could use some help.

So much puke. I need backup.

"Shit," he muttered.

I reached over him, tapped the lower case "i" on the right side of the screen, and swiped off the mute function.

"Maybe don't put your wife on Do Not Disturb?"

"Oh, I didn't realize—"

I sighed and flopped over to my side, facing away from him. My heart felt fragile, ready to shatter into a million pieces. I kept telling myself that *I* was crazy, that things were fine and we were going through a rough patch.

But . . .

This didn't feel like a rough patch. It felt like—

I bit my lip hard, stopping the thought before it could completely materialize.

We'd worked through tough times before. Every couple had ups and downs. What made us different was that we could talk to each other about anything.

Or we used to, anyway.

I turned my head so I could see him over my shoulder. "Not realizing things seems to be the theme with you lately, Rob. Can we talk about what's going on? It's not like you to be so detached."

Silence.

He sat six inches away from me, eyes on his phone, and he didn't even look at me.

He. Didn't. Look. At. Me.

In that moment, I felt ten years old again. Begging my mom to see me. To want me. To value me.

And in that moment, I hated my husband for making me feel that way.

I wasn't that little girl any longer. I knew my own worth. I—

Didn't beg for love. That came internally. I loved myself.

Because Rob had given me the strength to learn how.

His touch made me jump.

It was a gentle caress, one soft brush of his thumb beneath my eye to collect a drop of moisture I hadn't realized was there.

"Miss, I—"

His phone rang. He glanced down at it, and I held my breath, waiting for him, *wishing* he would decline it.

He didn't.

His finger swiped across the screen.

"Hello?" Rob said and walked from the room.

7

"*B*ye, Mom!" Max yelled the next day as he jumped out of the car and headed for his classroom.

"Love you!" I called through the open window.

"Love you, too!" he called back.

I smiled and pulled out of the drop-off line, soaking up the sentiment even as I recognized that the little boy I was raising wasn't so little anymore.

"You're next, Allie."

"Okay, Mom," she said, then went right back to humming the ABCs.

"Feeling all better?"

"Mmmhmm." A pause. "I miss Daddy."

"I know, honey," I said, even as my heart squeezed tightly. I missed her dad as well. "But he's working hard to keep everyone safe."

"From the bad guys?"

"Yup." I nodded, and when we stopped at a signal—one of five in the entire town—I met her eyes in the rearview mirror. "Daddy has an important job, but he loves us very much. Did you know he snuck in after you were asleep last night and tucked you in?"

She smiled, brown eyes widening. "He tucked Mr. Tails under my arm."

Mr. Tails was the rainbow stuffed cat Allie carried with her everywhere. She'd had it since she was a baby and though it was definitely tattered, she loved it.

Mr. Tails was also currently buckled into the seat next to Allie.

Safety first, in our family.

"He sure did, and he always puts your blankets just right, doesn't he?"

"Yup."

The light turned, and I pulled forward. "Should we sing a song before your school?"

"The Silly Pizza Song!"

I groaned. "Again?"

"Again!"

I laughed, but since this was our routine, the song was already cued up on my phone. I pressed play, and the song blared through the car's speakers.

We sang about crackers and candy and banana-topped pizza until it was time to drop Allie at school.

Back at home, I finished throwing the kids' sheets and blankets that remained from the previous day's Operation Plague into the washer before sitting down with my laptop and a cup of coffee in the kitchen. I pulled up my blog, replied to comments, checked that the next several posts were cued up to publish automatically, and wrote a quick check-in about the drama of the previous day.

At least being sick had the benefit of providing me blog material.

I shared my latest recipe video to Facebook, then a pretty and stylized shot of the finished product to Instagram.

When the business part was done, I finally got to do my favorite thing.

Cook.

In honor of yesterday, I made soup.

Not standard-issue, bland chicken noodle soup, but hearty, filling, and a little-bit-spicy-sweet potato with rice, carrots, and kale chicken soup.

It was delicious, and I found myself sampling, then breaking down and heating up a loaf of homemade sourdough to go with it. I scooped up a large helping, buttered several slices of bread, and ate my first peaceful meal in what felt like an eternity.

Each bite brought something slightly different to my palate. The creaminess of the cooked sweet potatoes, a little explosion of brightness when parsley landed on my tongue. Salty, tangy, savory, the crunch of the sourdough's crust when I dipped it in the soup, and just a hint of sweetness when I got a bite with everything all at once.

I ate the entire bowl. Plus, half the loaf of sourdough.

My phone chimed as I was styling a bowl for photographs.

"Hello?" I answered, distracted as I sprinkled an artistic arrangement of crumbs next to the spoon. I'd taken a bite from one last slice—someone had to do the hard work—and placed it on a pretty blue plate next to the bowl of soup. That way I could link both recipes on my website.

"Miss!" My sister's panicked voice exploded through the airwaves.

My stomach clenched, mind reeling at what could have happened. Was Abby okay? "What is it?"

"I burned dinner!"

I laughed, relief coursing through me.

"It's not funny."

"Kel, you *always* burn dinner."

"Well, I have no backup plan and Rosa is on vacation."

"It's only one o'clock," I said, adjusting the angle of the bowl and spoon before snapping a few photos. "You've got hours. Order a pizza. Or defrost something from the freezer. I know Rosa stocked it for you."

Rosa was Kelly's husband's housekeeper. She'd been with the Roosevelt family since Justin was a child and was an awesome cook. She was also getting very close to retiring, which meant that those days were coming to an end.

"I can't," Kel said.

"Why not? Or have Justin bring something home."

Kel sighed. "He offered, and I got all mad."

I snorted. "Kel . . ."

"I know. I *know* I can't cook, but then he got all superior about having someone cater this, and I just lost it."

My phone between my ear and shoulder, I took a few more shots then put my camera down. "Cater what?"

"Justin has work people coming over tonight, and I—"

"Wanted to impress him?"

Kel huffed. "Yes."

"You know you already married him, right?"

I felt her eyes roll through the phone. "Doesn't mean I don't want to impress him."

Yeah. I knew the feeling.

"Okay, I have to grab the kids, but as long as you don't mind the monsters coming with me, I'll bring by some ingredients and we can cook together."

"Are they recovered?"

"We're more than twenty-four hours in the clear, but if you'd rather not risk Abby getting sick, I can just drop by some stuff for you to heat up."

And hopefully not burn.

"Hmm." Kel was quiet for a moment. "No, I'd probably ruin that too. If the kids were well enough to go to school, I'm sure they're good to come."

"Sure?" I asked.

"New mom jitters," Kelly said. "I'm sure."

"Okay." I did a little jig in the kitchen. I was going to cook for new people, and that made me happy. "How many and any allergies?"

"Six people including Justin and me, and, um . . ."

"You don't know about allergies?" I asked, filling in the pause.

"I didn't ask."

"Okay, *ask*. And then text me. I'll stop by the store on the way over."

We hung up, and I bustled around the kitchen, packing up the soup, downloading my photographs from the memory card and onto my laptop. I'd bring my camera with me, knowing this too would give me good material for a blog post.

How often did I cater events?

Never.

Not that cooking dinner for six people really counted, but I was excited for the chance to try out some new things.

I portioned the soup into containers and put them in the freezer before running out the door to pick Allie up from school.

"Did you have a nice day?" I asked while we meandered back to the car. We had thirty minutes before I had to get Max. Enough time to do . . . basically nothing.

"Uh-huh." A pause. "I'm hungry."

My lips twitched at the familiar exchange. She wouldn't dish on the details of school until she had a little food in her belly. "I've got a snack for you in the car."

"Yay!"

Hunger forgotten, or perhaps more acute, Allie picked up the pace and sprinted for the car.

Minivan.

It was a minivan.

I'd gotten to the point in my life where I drove a minivan.

Rolling my eyes at myself, I pushed a few buttons on the key fob to remotely start it and then opened the side door.

Minivan or not, those perks were good.

Allie found the thermal pack I'd put on the floor in front of her car seat and quickly unzipped it.

"Swatermfelon!" she shouted before shoving a piece into her mouth. "I rofe swatermfelon!"

Of course I had to translate that—"I love watermelon!"—since her mouth was full, but I knew my baby girl.

And she loved all fruit, most especially watermelon.

"We'll get Max, stop at the grocery store, then head for Aunt Kelly's, okay?"

Allie paused in her inhalation of the melon. "Did she burn something again?"

I laughed as I buckled her in. "What do you think?"

"Definitely."

8

"So what are we making again?" Kelly asked, her eyes wide as she surveyed the mass of bags on her kitchen counter.

"It's basically chicken, rice, and veggies," I said as I unpacked ingredients and began lining everything up.

"Oh."

"It's *fancy* chicken, rice, and veggies, okay?"

Kel sighed in relief. "Okay."

I peeked out the kitchen window, watching the kiddos play with Henry, who was Kel's best friend from high school. He was also a very good chef in his own right and worked at the local restaurant his family owned.

"You sure Henry doesn't mind watching Max and Allie?"

"Nope. He wanted some time away from the diner, and the kids are a good distraction."

I raised a brow at that very nondescript explanation. Kel put her hands up. "Not my story to tell."

"Hmm." I gathered the canvas shopping bags, folding them up and setting them on the counter. "And why didn't you hit him up to cook?"

"I did," Kelly said. "He wouldn't bail me out."

I bumped her shoulder, nodding at the sink so she could wash up. "I see how it is, I'm second best?"

"That's not—"

"Second best," I sing-songed, walking over to where Abby was stacking blocks in a playpen in the corner of the kitchen. It was shoved between the wall and a wood table and chairs, one of which looked a little lopsided. "Just like this chair," I said as I pushed it out of the way and smacked a kiss on Abby's head.

"Your eyes"—emerald green just like her daddy's—"are gorgeous."

The water turned off, and Kelly came over, drying her hands with a towel. "They are. I thought she might look like Rex, and then . . ."

"Justin is her dad, Kel. Not Rex." I put an arm around her shoulders. "You have the papers to prove it."

"I wish I hadn't—"

"You made a mistake, but you got something precious and valuable from it, yeah?"

Kel nodded, and I went for levity.

"Plus, it's good you chose to make a mistake with twins because it makes explanations a lot easier."

Kel had previously been in a relationship with Justin's twin, Rex, and had ended up pregnant and alone . . . at least until Justin had showed up in Darlington.

They'd hit a few bumps but had eventually figured it out. Or I'd thought so anyway.

"Are you unhappy?" I asked, taking in her pale face and the lines around her mouth. "You don't have to stay with—"

"I'm not unhappy," Kel said. "I'm freaked out."

Abby had been thoroughly entertained with her wooden blocks, but at the sound of her mom's worried voice extended her arms. "Up, mama."

"Why?" I asked as Kelly swept her from the playpen.

"I'm pregnant again."

I shrieked. "What?"

"I know." Kelly hugged Abby tightly before the little girl squirmed to be put down.

"But—but *how*?" I shook my head. "Okay, don't answer that." I crossed back to the kitchen island and began washing vegetables.

Kel giggled. "No details?"

I wrinkled my nose as I began chopping onions. "No, thanks."

My sister corralled Abby in the kitchen as I moved on to chopping carrots and lettuce. I peeled some potatoes, trimmed some asparagus, and then set all the veggies to the side. "So are we celebrating?"

"Justin doesn't know yet," she said, biting her lip. "I—uh . . . we moved so quickly with Abby and the wedding and now . . ."

I put the knife down. "That's not what has you worried." I fixed her with a glare. "Spill."

"What if he loves her less?" Kel asked. The question was quiet and almost drowned out by Abby's babbling of "Ma! Ma! Ma!"

"Oh, Kel." I crossed around the island and sat down on the floor in front of Abby. The sweet little girl crawled into my lap and tugged at my hair. "How could anyone not love her?"

"She's not his. Or not entirely anyway."

"Bullshit."

Kelly and Abby both stared up at me with wide eyes. I sent up a silent prayer that the little parrot wouldn't pick that moment to begin mimicking me.

Her first curse word courtesy of Aunt Melissa. Yeah, that would be awesome.

"Justin loves her. He loves you."

"But what if he thinks it's too soon."

"He won't."

Kel sighed and sat back onto her heels. "How do you know?"

I smiled. "I know."

"But *how*?"

I took my sister's face in my hands and turned it to the doorway, where Justin stood. His face was a little pale, his eyes a little wide, but he was grinning.

"Is it true?" he asked.

Kel bit her lip and nodded shyly.

Justin was across the room in a few short strides, scooping Abby up, and then pulling Kelly into his arms. "How are you feeling?" he asked fiercely.

"Fine. Not sick at all," Kelly said. "Or not yet anyway."

He smiled and hugged them tightly as I backed slowly away. I'd give them a few minutes before I went back and finished cooking dinner.

Justin's voice trailed after me as I slipped out onto the front porch. "I'm not going to call you an idiot, but what were you thinking? I love you both so, so much."

And, *ding*, that was the correct answer. Good job, Justin.

Henry and the kids were running like maniacs over the front lawn, tagging each other and then sprinting away, giggling and falling all over the place. Adorable little monkeys.

I slipped back inside, found the kitchen empty, and got back to work. The thought of another baby made me smile. I loved babies. They were so squishy and fluffy and smelled yummy.

Okay, I knew I was weird.

I didn't want another one for myself, but I did like the idea of being an auntie again.

Most of the perks but less of the work.

Smiling to myself, I got back to my own work. From what Kelly had told me, the clients were coming over at five thirty. I threw together a quick appetizer of brie, cranberries, and candied walnuts then sliced up and toasted another loaf of my sourdough bread, deciding that my sister owed me big time for parting with my favorite snack.

Maybe I'd put her on babysitting duty for the monsters. Rob and I hadn't had a date night since—

I couldn't remember.

Frowning, I sliced herbs and mixed them with butter, then

pounded the chicken breasts until they were very thin. I spread the herb butter over the surface before rolling up each piece and searing it in a pan. It would give the chicken a little color—anemic-looking food did not taste yummy—and some nice texture.

And though I snapped pictures each step of the way, my mind was on autopilot. When *was* the last time I'd spent some time alone with my husband that wasn't a half hour on the couch before I fell asleep?

Years.

It had literally been years since I'd been on a date with Rob.

A knot loosened in my chest. Well, that was clearly the issue. We'd grown apart. But I could fix that. I could eliminate the distance between us, and we could go back . . . find ourselves again.

It was so simple.

We needed a date night.

I rolled my eyes. We needed more than a date night, but spending some time alone together would be the first step across that bridge. I would call Callie and set up a time in the next couple of weeks.

"Okay," I murmured, sliding the pan with the chicken into the oven to finish cooking. "I can do this."

We could get back on track. We *had* to. I glanced out the window at the little monsters now collapsed on the grass, pointing up at the clouds in the sky. I could picture their voices calling out the shapes, knew that I would do literally anything for them.

I could fix my marriage.

For them.

For me.

9

I'd just sat down to my laptop after dropping the kiddos at school the next morning when my phone rang.

"Hello?" I answered without looking.

"You're a goddess."

My lips twitched at my sister's voice. "Tell me more."

Kelly laughed, but her voice was sincere. "Thank you, Miss. For bailing me out."

"And for writing a full page of instructions that even you couldn't mess up." I'd finished up the food, leaving it all to warm in the oven, before gathering the kiddos and scooting home.

"Hmpf," my sister said, then sighed. "Okay fine, it's true. And the MacAlisters loved your food. I was going to take credit for it all, but then I knew I'd have to attempt to replicate it and—" Abby shrieked in the background. "Hold on."

I listened to Kel gather up Abby, sounds muffled as she attempted to hold toddler and phone alike. When she came back on, she was panting.

"I—ouch. That's Mommy's hair, Abby-girl. I just want to—*ow* —tell your auntie something."

"Want to call me back later?" I asked as I went through some photographs from the previous night. "Oh, did you happen to take any pictures of the prepared plates? I forgot to take some."

A pause. "It wasn't on the instruction sheet."

I grinned, tapped a few keys on my laptop. "So that's a no. It's okay, I guess my mind was somewhere else."

"You could always make it again," my sister said, way too innocent. "It'd be a real struggle, but I could be employed to make sure it didn't go to waste."

"Nice try," I said and glanced at the clock. I needed to get off the phone in the next couple of minutes. I was volunteering in Max's class in addition to my normal work stuff, and time was already tight. "What did you want to tell me?"

"Oh! So Tammy MacAlister is the wife of Justin's work colleague. I guess their fathers invested in the same tech start-up or something, and now the boys are trying to figure out if they want to put more capital into the business."

I struggled to prevent my eyes from glossing over. "Okay."

"But that's not the exciting thing," Kel said.

"What is the *exciting thing*?"

"Tammy works for that food channel. You know the one on TV with all the celebrity chefs, and she loved your food. Like, *loved* it. Raved about it." Kelly was talking fast, and my heart was pounding, blood swooshing past my ears as I tried to process what my sister was telling me. "And then I showed her your blog and Instagram—which damn, I didn't realize you had ten thousand followers, Miss! That's amazing."

I held my breath.

"Melissa?"

I released it, strived for a calm voice. "I'm here."

"She wants to meet you. She wants to run a camera test and see some more of your food and—"

"Holy arancini."

"I know—what?"

I collapsed back against my chair. "They're fried balls of rice.

Italian. Super delicious." I waved my hand through the air. "Never mind that. How? *When*? I—"

"I told Tammy I would pass along your information to her if it was something you were interested in."

That gave me pause.

Okay, not really. Because *this*—a cooking show! Eek! It was something I'd always fantasized about, but had never believed was remotely possible.

"Yes, please," I said calmly.

"Can we squee now?" my sister asked.

"Oh my God," I said. "I hope so."

And then we squeed.

———

AFTER KELLY and I completed our squeal-fest and hung up, I fired off a quick text to Rob.

Call me when you can. I need to tell you something!

I settled in for the long haul, editing pictures, finding the perfect descriptive words for my soup recipe from yesterday. Of course, I shared a few more details of our recovery from the Plague—not too much, because it was a food blog, after all—but I did think my readers liked it when I let them in to my own life a little.

And the sick kids, dog eating my shoe, it was too real not to share. I purposely didn't say funny, either. It was too soon after the plague to be funny—

My poor shoes.

But I fully expected to be able to laugh about it all in approximately . . . eight and a half decades.

Snorting, I scheduled the post then moved on to selecting which photograph would look best on Instagram when my phone rang.

I lurched for it, thinking it could be Tammy and all my cooking show dreams, but it was Rob.

Which was almost as good.

"Hi!" I said. "I've got the best—"

Wind wove through the speaker, rattling against my eardrums. "Are the kids okay?"

I stiffened at the shortness in his voice. "They're fine. Why?"

"You said to call."

"I need to tell you something. I have really awesome news—"

A voice intruded on their conversation. "Sorry. You'll have to tell me later," Rob said. "I need to go."

"But—"

"I'm at work, Miss."

"Yeah." I paused, throat tightening, eyes tearing up.

"Bye."

Before I'd opened my mouth to reply in kind, he'd hung up.

My heart twisted, aching as though it had been stabbed. I tried to tell myself that his job was dangerous. Important. That my text had been ambiguous so he'd called right away.

Because he'd been worried. He cared.

But he hadn't asked about me.

And the voice on the other end of the phone, the one that had barely reached my ears over the wind and noise, was female.

10

*R*ob hung up the phone and glanced over at Celeste as he slipped back into the car. "Good?" he asked.

She clucked her tongue. "Wife calling when you're at work. So cliché."

No, he thought. What was cliché was his wife calling when he was with his *girlfriend*.

Fake girlfriend, but cliché nonetheless.

"Okay, so what do we know about this building?"

Celeste straightened, all traces of femininity vanishing from her voice as she began listing what the surveillance of the last few weeks had discovered.

Which, unfortunately, wasn't much.

"So we've been watching this place for weeks and haven't seen a single shipment come in or out? Haven't witnessed a deal?" He shook his head. "Why are we wasting our time here?"

She tapped a finger—complete with bright-red polish—to her lips. Melissa would never wear something so flashy. His wife wasn't about upkeep. She liked things simple and underdone.

Skirts with flowers. Lacy shirts. Jeans and flats mixed with the occasional pair of sweats.

No heels. Nothing ostentatious.

Not like Celeste.

Even in the department-required button-down and slacks, she oozed sex.

"They're doing something here," Celeste said. "I can feel it. I just don't know if they've moved operations because we're keeping an eye on things or if we haven't figured out all the moving parts yet."

"And our source says he got the drugs here?"

"Not exactly. He said that all his dealers dried up. Refused to sell to him again until he got clearance from the boss."

"And the boss was here."

Celeste nodded.

Rob sighed and stared out the windshield at the nondescript warehouse on the outskirts of Darlington.

He didn't want this shit within a thousand miles of his family, let alone the twenty between this building and downtown Darlington.

Tri-Hills was supposed to be a family-friendly community, a place that was safe for kids to wander, for the elderly to not have to worry about being mugged or assaulted or their homes being broken into.

He worried that times were changing, that the town he'd grown up in wouldn't be the same for his kids.

Which was life, he supposed, but not what he wanted for *his* family.

"All right," he said. "Let's keep up the surveillance. But we'll run your idea by the chief."

Celeste squealed then leaned up as though to kiss him on his cheek. "You're the best, Robbie!"

He dodged, turning on the car before reversing out of the alley and heading back for the station.

Celeste chattered on about her plan to take down the dealer, expanding on some good trains of thought and doing a very thorough job of brainstorming by herself since he wouldn't be able to get a word in edgewise with her current mood.

Not that he wanted to.

He was more focused on the smear of red lipstick on his collar.

was in a mood.

A bad one.

And for no other reason than my blueberry pie recipe was off.

The kids were in bed, close enough to sleep that they wouldn't be coming out because they needed another cup of water or their light wasn't bright enough, or one of the multitude of other reasons their creative little minds came up with.

Rob was asleep on the couch, the TV a soft murmur that barely reached the kitchen.

And my pie was off.

It wasn't the crust. *That* was tender, salty, and slightly sweet. Perfect. It was something in the filling, something that tasted off.

I popped an unused blueberry from the bowl into my mouth. Tangy but not bad. The butter was fresh, as was the cream. I'd picked them up from the store that morning.

Maybe it was the eggs?

"Hey."

I whirled around and saw Rob leaning against the doorway of the kitchen.

"Hey," I said, setting down the carton I'd picked up to check the expiration date.

"You're up late."

He didn't move from his position. Once he might have come over, taken me in his arms, teased me about my obsession over the pie, then kissed me until I forgot all about recipes and blueberries and fresh eggs.

"I don't have the plague any longer," I blurted.

He raised a brow. "What?"

"Never mind." Why had I said that? Why was I scared as hell to tell him that I might have a chance at a cooking show? That *I*, a small-town girl who'd married young and not amounted to much might have a chance to realize my dream? Why couldn't I tell him, ask him to hold me close and tell me everything would be all right?

Why couldn't I find a way to breach the wall that had been erected between us?

"Meliss—"

"How's work going?" I asked.

Three words that closed him up tighter than a vault. His face flattened out—no emotion, no twinkle in his eyes. "Fine."

"I—uh. Okay." I turned back to the eggs, blinking rapidly, but I managed to get a look at the expiration date. Which was several weeks in the future.

So not the eggs, the milk, or butter. What the hell was wrong with my pie?

"You should go to bed."

I shrugged, surveying the counter. The answer must be a simple one. The pie wasn't inedible, just not quite right. "I've got to fix this."

The pie.

My marriage.

"Why?" Rustling came from the doorway, and I turned, heart skipping a beat as he walked toward me. "It's just a pie."

Perhaps it was.

But it wasn't *just* a recipe gone wrong. Somehow this had become about everything that had gone wrong with our relationship over the last few months. The slow rot, trailed by the rapid disintegration of our communication. Maybe we'd been lazy, too comfortable in our ways. Relationships took work, and we'd sat back on our laurels too much, assumed that everything would always be good. That when it wasn't, we would still find a way through.

But I was at a loss now.

I kept bumping into that brick wall, unable to find my way over, under, through, or around.

And, frankly, I was almost tired of trying.

"It's not just a pie," I snapped. "This matters to me, and I know that you've been wrapped up in whatever has been happening at the department lately, but this"—I waved my hand at the kitchen—"is important to me."

My chest heaved as I waited for him to respond.

Except, he didn't.

Silence stretched as we stood three feet apart, a visually perfect slice of blueberry pie on a plate, ready to be photographed.

The distance between us may have been the Grand Canyon for all that I was able to cross it. He didn't know about the cooking show, or rather, the possibility of one. I hadn't wanted to tell him in front of the kids, in case things didn't pan out. We'd eaten dinner together, and he'd taken the kids up for a bath and books while I'd done the dishes.

It was all very routine. When he was home, he did bedtime then relaxed with a show while I cooked.

Sometimes I propped my iPad up in the kitchen to catch up on the latest Netflix craze or Rob sat with me while I worked, acting the part of official taste-tester.

But more often than not of late, he hadn't been home to play that role.

He sighed. "I get that it's important to you, but the pie isn't life or death."

"Of course not." My eyes dropped to the floor, one that Rob and I had laid together. It wasn't perfect but it did the job.

I almost snorted. If that wasn't an analogy for our current circumstances . . .

Silence.

"I'm not happy," is what I wanted to say.

I didn't get the chance.

Rob turned and walked away. "Try not to stay up too late with your *pie.*"

"WHAT AM I GOING TO DO?" I said into the phone two days later. Or shrilled, more precisely. If shrilled was a verb, which I hoped it was, since that was all my brain could come up with.

"What, Miss?" Kelly asked, distracted.

I could hear Justin's voice in the background—murmurs punctuated by soft laughter—and had an idea why she was distracted.

Normally I'd hang up, because gross. Today I was freaking out.

"She's going to be here in ten minutes, and I'm not ready!"

The kids were at school. Tammy, the wife of Justin's colleague and the food channel producer, was due any moment. And I hadn't done—

"Switch to FaceTime."

"What?"

Kel sighed, and my phone began trilling with that distinctive chirp. Automatically, I swiped, accepting the call. My sister's smiling face appeared on the screen. Justin was behind her, resting his head on one of her shoulders.

"You look beautiful," she said and Justin nodded in agreement. "That is the perfect Melissa outfit."

I glanced down at my jeans and blouse and my second favorite pair of flats. "You think? It's not too casual?"

"No. Perfect," Kel said firmly. "Where's the dog?"

"At puppy daycare."

"Good." She nodded. "Contain the little monster. Okay, show it to me."

"Show you what?"

"The spread."

I bit my lip and turned the camera around, moving the phone to give her a glimpse of the entire kitchen table filled with food. Including another blueberry pie that was perfect this time. Turned out I'd forgotten lemon juice last time around and it wasn't until after midnight when I'd spotted the yellow fruit perched next to the bowl, that I'd realized.

Kelly gasped. "Holy hell, Melissa. That's incredible."

I shrugged. "It's nothing—"

"You're crazy, now stop. Tammy will love you—" The doorbell rang.

"Oh God," I hissed. "She's here."

"Then let her in," Kel said. "I love you. You're awesome." I was just hanging up when she blurted, "Bring the leftovers later!"

Snorting, I hit the red button, pocketed my phone, and rushed to the front door.

12

*T*ammy MacAlister was a perky redhead with bright blue eyes. Her smile was warm.

"Come on in," I told her. "Can I get you a drink?"

"Water is fine," she said and followed me into the kitchen. "Oh my."

I winced, facing her. "I got a little carried away."

"This is beautiful." She crossed to the table. "Soup. Sandwiches. Pasta salad. Blueberry pie. If it tastes as good as it looks, I'll be a thousand pounds before I leave."

I laughed, my nerves starting to relax. "No guarantees," I told her as I grabbed a glass and filled it with a pitcher of my infused—strawberry, orange, and mint—water. "Please have a seat."

"There never are." But Tammy smiled and sat. "That's the problem with really good food."

I handed her the glass before taking the opposite chair. "I'm nervous," I blurted.

She grinned. "Me too. It's not often that I pick up my clients via my husband. But that chicken!"

"Good?" I asked, biting my lip.

"Delicious."

I blew out a breath. "I'm glad you enjoyed it. That recipe is one of my favorites and way too easy for as pretty as it looks."

"I did like the appearance the fresh herbs gave it," Tammy said. "Parsley and sage?"

I nodded. "Plus a little rosemary. Too much gives the chicken almost a soapy taste. A little hint brings out those savory notes without overpowering the flavor of everything else."

She nodded, and I wondered if I'd gone on one of my tangents. Sometimes I waxed poetic about food, to the eternal boredom of Rob and Kelly. But Tammy didn't seem bored. In fact, her eyes were warm when she said, "Tell me about your blog."

"How about we eat while I tell you?" I asked. "That way the soup doesn't get cold."

Tammy winked. "I like the way you think."

I grabbed a bowl and scooped up some chicken soup for her then filled a plate with a little bit of everything—a finger sandwich, pasta salad, petite fours, pie. It was way too much food, but at least she could take a bite of all that I had to offer.

As she ate and I served up a plate for myself, I told her how I'd started the blog because I'd been slowly going insane when Max was an infant and wouldn't sleep during the night.

He'd only sleep upright and strapped to my chest. Which wasn't exactly conducive for *my* sleep.

So instead of wallowing, I'd taken to cooking.

At least when I was a zombie the following evening from lack of sleep, dinner had already been made. By the time both of my kids were sleeping through the night, I'd had a stack of recipes but my body was used to being up half the night.

I'd played around with plating and taking pictures and had finally taken the social media plunge.

The rest was history.

"I remember those days," Tammy said. "Being so tired that you could hardly think straight."

"Being a mom is hard," I agreed. "Easier on the sleep part now, but harder in different ways."

Tammy tilted her head in question.

"They fight. All the time."

She smiled. "I only have the one, so I didn't get to experience that particular joy of motherhood."

"You're not missing out," I said. "Trust me."

We laughed, and then a quiet descended. I tried to give off some semblance of a calm, put together TV personality, but inside my nerves began to roil again. I'd given the background, she'd tasted my food. Next would come judgment.

"Your kitchen is beautiful."

I blinked then smiled. "My husband and I redid it ourselves."

"Really?"

I glanced at the cabinets that Rob had refinished a bright white, the tile backsplash and floor we'd installed.

"Really. With the exception of the countertops, we did it all." I shrugged. "Luckily it was all cosmetic—electricity and plumbing I draw the line at."

"I would too." Her laughter was bright and contagious, and I finally *finally* chilled.

This is going to be what it is, Miss, I thought, my pulse steadying. *You can't control everything.*

"Okay," Tammy said. "Ready to hear how these things normally work?"

I nodded. "Yes, please."

Tammy smiled as she pulled out her phone, snapping a few pictures of the spread. "I discuss you with my bosses, show them your blog, go on and on about how good your food is, and then we fly you to New York for a screen test."

My eyes were wide. "New York?"

Broadway. High rises. The subway. And *food*. So. Much. Food.

"Yup." She touched my hand and stood. "I'll be in touch once I talk to my bosses, and then we'll figure out a few days that work with your schedule to get you to New York. Sound good?"

I bobbed my head, pushing to my own feet. "That sounds fabulous."

We walked to the front door, and Tammy gave me a hug before she left. "It was such a pleasure to meet you."

"You as well. Safe travels."

Once she'd gotten into her car, I retreated to the kitchen and leaned back against the counter.

A screen test? New York? How was this real life?

I stayed there for a few minutes, frozen in shocked delight. And then I called my sister and we squealed.

After that very appropriate display of glee—occasionally we were allowed to act like teenagers, right?—I began packing up the leftover food. I'd take it to Kelly and Justin's house before I grabbed the kids from school.

Payment for services rendered. Or for being an awesome sister.

Twenty minutes later, I was loading up her fridge when my phone rang.

It was a local number, but one I didn't recognize.

"Hello?"

I could barely hear anything—it was all static and wind and voices.

"Hello?" I said again.

"I can't tell my wife . . ."

My heart twisted at the sound of Rob's voice.

"I've got two kids. This is about them . . ."

Knees trembling, I leaned back against the counter when the call suddenly went crystal clear, wind and static gone. Rob's voice came through with perfect clarity.

"No. She's nothing."

Click.

The call ended, and I glanced down at my phone.

Nothing.

Nothing.

My eyes slid closed, my legs trembled.

Nothing.

I jumped when my phone rang again, and I swiped to answer,

putting it up to my ear without looking at the ID.

"Ms. Mitchell?"

My voice wavered as I spoke. "Yes, this is her."

"Hi, this is Sandy from Bow Wow Patrol, and I, um, don't know how to tell you this . . ."

My eyes flashed open, and my stomach dropped. Oh God, what had Rocco done?

"Rocco escaped the outside enclosure, and we can't find him anywhere."

My knees gave out, and I sank to the floor, head dropping back to lean against the cabinets of Kel's kitchen.

"How long has he been missing?" I asked, shoving Rob to the back of my mind.

"Just about an hour."

I nodded though Sandy couldn't hear me, glancing at the clock and mentally making a plan. "I'm just outside of town. I'll stop by my house to double check he didn't somehow make his way home and then be there."

That would give me about forty-five minutes of search time before I had to pick up Allie from school.

Hopefully, it would be enough.

13

*I*t wasn't enough time.

Kelly was at a doctor's appointment—her first visit, and I didn't want to ruin what should be a happy moment—so I rushed across town and grabbed Allie from school. We drove to Bow Wow Patrol. Sandy met us outside, breathless and covered in leaves.

"We found him!" she said. "But he's—" Her eyes trailed over my shoulder to where Allie stood and the words cut off. "H-U-R-T."

My stomach clenched. Hard.

"Bad?"

A nod.

"What's bad, Mommy?" Allie asked.

I crouched in front of her and rested my hands on her shoulders. "Rocco got a little boo-boo, but he'll be okay," I said, hoping it would be true.

Standing, I turned to Sandy. "Where is he?"

"In the back."

I nodded before handing my phone to Allie. "Why don't you have a seat in the lobby and watch some videos?"

"Okay!" She snagged it and scampered for the automatic

sliding door leading into the doggy daycare, Sandy and I trailing after her, talking quietly.

"How bad?" I asked.

"I think his leg is broken, and he has some cuts that need cleaning." She paused, glancing over at Allie, who was now perched in a chair and thoroughly engrossed in the phone. "I found him at the bottom of a ravine."

"Wait here, honey, okay?" I said when Sandy pulled open the door to the back.

The receptionist gave me a sympathetic smile and nodded at Allie. "I'll keep an eye on her."

"Thanks," I murmured before following Sandy back.

And my heart broke.

"Oh, poor baby," I crooned, dropping to my knees inside the room where Rocco was. He was wrapped in a blanket, and the parts of him that I could see were covered in scratches and abrasions.

He shifted, trying to stand, and cried out in pain.

"I'm sorry, sweetheart. I'm so sorry," I said softly, continuing to talk to him as I pulled the blanket back and examined his leg.

My throat went tight at the angle—the *wrong* angle—of the bones. I needed to get him to the vet right away. I reached for my phone before realizing it was currently occupied by Allie. "Can I borrow your phone?" I asked Sandy.

"I called Dr. Johnson a few minutes ago. They'll be ready for you as soon as you get there." She sighed. "I don't know how he got out. We've pulled all the dogs inside and are inspecting the fence. I'm so sorry."

I pushed to my feet. "Thank you for finding him. It would have been—" My voice cracked and I blinked rapidly. "Thank you."

Sandy nodded before helping me carry Rocco out to my car. We got him settled then I returned to the lobby for Allie. "Thank you for being so patient, sweetheart," I said as we walked outside. "Rocco needs to see the vet, so we're going there next."

Allie's light brown eyes went wide. "Will he be okay?"

"Of course." I stroke her baby soft cheek. "He's got a couple of big boo-boos, but the vet will fix him right up." I got her buckled into her car seat, sent a silent prayer that my words would be true, and drove to the vet's office.

The moment my car pulled into the lot, Dr. Johnson came through the doors, scooping Rocco up and carrying him inside.

Allie and I spoke to Jane, the receptionist, before picking Max up from school. Luckily, Kelly was home from her appointment by the time we were heading back to our house, and she zipped over to hang with the kids.

It was only when I was back over to the vet's office that I realized I hadn't called Rob.

Nothing.

The word, said with a dismissive tone I'd never heard in my husband's voice before, blared through my mind.

And he loved Rocco. How would he react to his dog being hurt on my watch? Because of something that *I'd* wanted to do. I'd shoved Rocco into daycare and hadn't bothered to keep him safe.

I slid my phone back into my pocket.

Jane smiled when I came through the doors. "I was just going to call you."

A smile was good, right? It meant Rocco would be okay?

The dog destroyed my shoes and wreaked havoc with the best of them, but I still loved him.

"How is he?"

"Pretty banged up, but Dr. Johnson has the specifics for you. He's waiting in exam room three."

At her nod, I slipped past the desk and walked down the hall, knocking before pushing into the room with a three posted outside the door. Rocco was curled on a pile of blankets, looking very drowsy but a lot more comfortable than when I'd dropped him off.

He sported a cast on his back right leg and a myriad of bald spots where they must have shaved him to clean out his cuts. A blue compression bandage was wrapped around one front leg, white gauze peeking out from beneath it.

"Oh, poor Rocco," I said, and crouched down next to him.

"It looks worse than it is," Dr. Johnson said, appearing like a ninja in the doorway that led to the restricted back area for staff and patients only.

He was holding a file but set it aside to crouch next to us, giving Rocco a little scratch under his chin.

"Rocco's a lucky boy. He had a few spots that needed stitches, mainly on his legs and head, as his fur protected him elsewhere." Rocco's eyebrows perked up at his name before he settled his head more firmly on his paws with a sigh. "There was a small fracture in the tibia of his right hind leg, but that should heal without issue."

"Okay," I said, the twisting in my gut settling slightly. "So he's okay?"

He nodded, a small smile curving his mouth up. "My only concern at this time is internal bleeding. From what Sandy told me, it seems like he had a pretty big fall."

"What?"

She'd told me they'd found him at the bottom of a ravine, but I hadn't put two and two together. My heart twisted further as I imagined him falling, scrambling to stay upright, crashing into rocks and sticks, hurting, scared—

I swallowed hard and closed my eyes for a long moment.

"He's okay," Dr. Johnson said.

I nodded, blinked to clear the tears.

"I'd like to keep him overnight for observation. His X-rays and ultrasound are clear, but just in case."

I nodded again. "Okay."

He stood up and grabbed the folder. "Stay with Rocco as long as you want. Just check in with Jane when you leave."

Rocco shifted, resting his head on my thigh, and Dr. Johnson slipped into the back, closing the door behind him.

I scratched Rocco's ears gently, allowing my eyes to commit every visible inch of his body—and his many injuries—to memory. I tucked those into my brain, to the section that was extremely good at holding on to guilt.

Those I'd rehash later, punishing myself until I felt I'd suffered enough to make up for his injuries.

Selfish. I'd acted like my mother, pawning my responsibility off onto someone else just so I could have my fun.

I'd had my fun.

And Rocco had gotten hurt.

And . . . it was my fault.

A tear trickled down my cheek, but I brushed it away. I didn't deserve to purge the emotions, didn't get to excise the guilt. I had promised myself that I wouldn't be like my mother. Not ever.

But look what had happened. I'd turned into exactly the kind of selfish bitch she was, and so I had to experience this guilt over and over and over again.

Until I learned. Until I was better. Until I had made up for it.

14

I heated up a meal from the freezer but I don't remember what it was that I actually ate. The kids didn't complain though so it must have been taco casserole, mac and cheese, or something with chicken tenders.

"He's going to be okay." Kelly squeezed my arm. She'd stayed for dinner but Justin was waiting for her, so she and Abby were heading out. She hugged me. Tight. "Just remember that."

Words wouldn't come to form a response, not when my imagination was reliving what poor Rocco had gone through, so I just nodded. He was only a dog. It shouldn't be bothering me so much. But Rocco was innocent, and he'd been at doggie daycare so I could have my meeting.

And Rob loved him.

I sighed. I loved the furball too.

Dammit.

I blinked hard.

"You know—" Kel winced and broke off when Abby yanked at a lock of her hair. She untangled little fingers and said, "I know you're really good at it, but sooner or later you have to shed that martyr cape and let the rest of the world help."

All the air left my lungs in a rush. "You don't know what you're talking about."

My sister—my *younger* sister's face was full of pity "Oh sweetie. I love you, but you're wrong."

"I'm—"

"No one is perfect," she said. "Or expects *you* to be." Abby let out a screech and Kelly smiled down at her daughter. "Time for bed, huh?"

She called out a goodbye and headed for her car.

"I know I'm not perfect," I muttered, closing the door and slumping forward to rest my forehead against the plank of wood.

"How about perfect for me?"

Rob's voice made me straighten and my eyes immediately fill with tears. I turned, regret pouring through me when the smile he'd been wearing slipped from his face.

My news would further cement that.

He was in uniform, his duty belt still around his waist. I'd always loved him in blues. He was the female fantasy come to life.

"What's wrong, babe?"

The question, filled with obvious concern and actual emotion for the first time in what felt like forever, coupled with him extending his arms, made me forget everything. The woman's voice in the background of the call, the way he'd said I was nothing, his distance, how he'd been so oblivious and missed so much.

I wanted those arms around me. I wanted that comfort.

I wanted my husband back.

With a sigh of relief, I stepped into his embrace. Tears slipped down my cheeks, dripping off my chin and pooling onto the collar of my shirt. With Rob, it had always been different. All the walls that existed to keep me safely distant weren't there with him.

But lately they'd crept in with my husband, and I didn't know how to stop building them.

Not when he kept hurting me.

Not when I allowed myself to *be* hurt without talking to him.

Yet in that moment, none of it mattered. I had my husband, my best friend, and he was there for me.

"Shh," he said, stroking the hair back from my face. "Whatever it is, it'll be okay."

"Why's Mommy crying?" Allie asked.

I sniffed, trying to quiet my sobs. I didn't want to upset her or Max.

"Mom?" Max asked, grabbing me around the leg.

"I-I'm okay," I said, my voice only slightly shaky. "Just a little upset."

"Why don't you guys go pick out your books, and I'll read to you tonight?" Rob said.

"Okay!" Allie started to run off before making a skidding turn and throwing her arms around me. "Love you!"

"Love you too, baby."

Max touched my arm, and I glanced down at him. He studied me for a long moment before nodding and pressing a kiss to my hand. "Love you, Mom."

"Love you too, buddy."

He ran upstairs.

Rob waited until the pounding footsteps had faded before he took my hand and led me toward the kitchen. "Okay, spill," he said, pushing me down in a chair then crouching in front of me.

"It's Rocco. He got out today and fell down a ravine. H-he broke his leg, and Dr. Johnson wants to keep him overnight in case of internal bleeding." I took a deep breath because my voice was getting shrill and my eyes were filling with tears again.

"How did he get out?"

It was a reasonable question. And also one I didn't want to answer.

"Sandy isn't sure," I hedged.

Rob raised a brow and sat back on his haunches. "Why would Sandy be unsure?" His tone was harder now, laced with no-nonsense cop.

"Because Rocco was at Bow Wow Patrol when he got out."

"Why?"

I hesitated.

"*Melissa.*"

"This isn't how I wanted to tell you." My eyes went to a spot over his right shoulder, mentally dissecting the kitchen clutter. I needed to sort the mail, finish the dishes—

"Melissa"—my gaze flashed back to his face, angry and dark —"you need to tell me what the fuck is going on."

I burst to my feet. "I wanted to tell you. I tried to tell you, but you blew me off."

"We talked last night."

"Gah! I hate it when you do that." I paced the floor we'd laid together and wasn't that memory a nice little slap in the face at a moment like this? "Nitpicking my words, tacking on little disclaimers so that you don't have to be wrong. *Yes*, we talked last night. *No*, you didn't give me enough of your precious time so that I could tell you what's been going on in my life."

He opened his mouth, closed it. Then he sighed and said, "I thought it was *our* life."

"It hasn't been *our* life for a long time." When he didn't reply, I said, "You might have been home with me and the kids in body, but your mind wasn't here, your heart wasn't and *hasn't* been here for months."

Silence.

"You pulled back, Rob, and I miss you."

For a second, I thought my husband might actually make an appearance. His eyes softened as he stood and crossed to me, lightly brushing his knuckles down my cheek when he got near.

Then his face closed down. "What haven't you told me?"

He might as well have slapped me. The words were cold, his expression tight and frigid.

I recited the facts in monotone. "I cooked for Justin's work colleague a few days ago. His wife is an executive at a cooking channel. She loved my food, checked out my blog and recipes, and asked to set up a meeting with me today. They want me to come to New York for a screen test."

"No."

I blinked, startled from my recitation. "What?"

"No. You can't go to New York for a screen test."

I stepped back.

Rob stepped forward.

I lifted my chin. "Why not?"

"Your place is here. The kids." He shook his head, turned away. "Rocco already got hurt because of this stupid idea—"

"Rocco getting hurt was an accident."

"Because of this woman and her meeting," he said, taking his own turn at pacing the floor. "He would have been at home if not for that."

"It's not Tammy's fault Rocco was injured."

"Fine," he snapped and thrust a hand through his hair. "It was *your* fault."

My stomach twisted, that wonderfully painful guilt flooding in. I held it close, let it batter me even as I pretended my husband's words hadn't cut me deep. "You're being unreasonable."

"You're being irresponsible."

I laughed. Laughed until my stomach hurt and tears threatened. I'd been called a lot of things in my life—by my mother, by jerky kids at school growing up, even by Kelly in her teenage years when I'd been more mom than sister.

But never by my husband.

"Irresponsible." A shake of my head. "That's bullshit, and you know it."

"I—"

The pounding of footsteps radiated through the floor above our heads and was punctuated by a resounding, "MOM!"

It also gave me the out that was needed. My insides felt like they'd been sliced by knives. I was exhausted. I was hurt and emotional and . . .

"Go read to our kids," I murmured.

For once, I didn't head to the fridge, didn't pull out ingredients and start cooking my pain away.

Instead, I grabbed a bottle of wine from the counter, a glass from the cupboard, and headed out the back door.

Some things just called for wine.

I didn't look back as I went through the door and settled myself into a chair on the deck. I didn't need to. This house and family were my everything, and I could track every movement without a wasted glance.

I heard Rob climb the stairs—not bothering to avoid the creaking one. I listened to the kids' muffled but clearly excited voices as they talked about their days. I watched the glow disappear from the deck as their lights were flicked off. I heard quiet footfalls descending . . . and that damned squeaky step again.

I heard Rob's car start up.

And drive away.

I finished the bottle of wine.

15

I woke up with a pounding headache and a violent urge for bacon, eggs, and hash browns.

Food would have to wait for aspirin to kick in though.

With a groan, I rolled to the side and saw the time.

Of course.

The kids were going to be late for school.

But that seemed slightly less important when I noticed that Rob's side of the bed was untouched. For all the years we'd been married, the only times he hadn't slept by my side were when he'd been on a night shift.

I guess that wasn't the case any longer.

Forcing my eyes from the neatly made half of the bed, from the pillow that was undented, I hustled into the closet.

No time for emotions and regrets.

My kids needed to get to school.

I brushed my teeth, threw my hair into a ponytail, and grabbed the first set of clothes my hands touched.

Three minutes for me being somewhat presentable to the rest of humanity might be a record.

I poked my head into the kids' bedrooms and, finding them

empty, rushed down the stairs, hopping over the creaking step, and skidding to a halt in the kitchen.

My sister was there, helping Allie into her backpack. Max was sitting on the floor, already wearing his, and playing with Abby.

Kelly glanced up and smiled. "After yesterday, I figured you might need relief this morning." She straightened the pack on Allie's shoulders. "Now you just turn around and go enjoy a nice long shower. I'm taking the kids to school. Dr. Johnson called your cell earlier and said Rocco would be ready to come home around noon."

My eyes flashed to the counter, and I saw my phone there. I guess I'd been so out of it the night before I hadn't brought it upstairs.

"Rocco!" Max yelled, making Abby laugh.

I smiled.

"I've got these guys today," my sister said. "You take care of getting the fluffball settled."

The tension in my gut eased. "You're a goddess."

Kel bowed. "I know. Go get in the car, munchkins," she said to the kids, raising her key fob and pressing a button. We watched through the kitchen window as the two doors to her minivan slid open. "Never thought I'd say it, but minivans rock." A grin. "Now, go spend an inordinate time on personal grooming while you have the chance."

"Breakfast?" I asked as she scooped up Abby.

"Done," Kel said as Max and Allie sprinted out the front door without a look back.

"Boosters?"

She nodded. "Justin installed them last night."

I let out a relieved sigh. "Thanks, sissy."

"Anytime." She hugged me and went outside.

I waved after she'd settled Abby into her seat, smiling when she pushed a button and the doors closed.

Minivans *did* rock.

Then I saw Rob's note propped next to the coffee pot, and my smile slipped away.

Will be at Henry's if you need me.

I CRUMPLED the paper and jammed it into the overflowing trashcan.

What the hell did that mean?

I grabbed a coffee cup and filled it. Was Rob hanging out for the morning? Is that where he'd spent last night?

Had he left and was staying there permanently?

No. We hadn't gotten to that point. Right?

Right?

Dammit. I hated this, I thought, bustling around the kitchen as irritation and fear and concern washed through me. I grabbed a package of blackberries and some homemade vanilla yogurt, layering it and the berries into a bowl before topping with a few scoops of granola.

I sat down at the table, spoon in hand but stomach no longer hungry.

There was so much between Rob and I—baggage, barriers, resentment—but we'd always been able to talk things out in the past. Except . . . maybe we'd never really dealt with it all.

I knew I'd done my fair share of ignoring the small stuff that I hadn't wanted to battle over, and God knew, I was good at boxing up emotions I didn't want to deal with.

Was this how marriages imploded? Too much compartmentalizing, too much ignoring of the problems and pretending that everything was okay?

No.

That wasn't us. This was just a rough patch. We'd get through. We always did.

I stood up, setting my bowl in the sink, and turned to head upstairs for a shower. But there was that trash again. The lid sat askew, papers spewing out onto the floor. Reminding me of everything that wasn't right in my life.

Ugh.

I shoved the garbage down angrily, slammed the top closed. "Couldn't he have at least taken the flipping trash out before he left?"

Left me.

Left us.

Then tears were in my eyes and dripping down my cheeks. I pretended they didn't exist as I climbed the stairs. I ignored them as they mingled with the warm water of the shower.

And, fancy that, my eyes were dry by the time my body was.

My heart, on the other hand, was bruised and aching.

———

"So he'll need the cast for a few weeks, then we'll take another X-ray, and if all is good, Rocco will be a free man." Dr. Johnson smiled as he patted Rocco on the head. "Or dog, rather."

"In the meantime, I've got to keep him calm?" I glanced at Rocco's tail, already tapping against the floor like a propeller spinning a million miles per hour.

The vet snorted, a lock of his dark brown hair falling forward over his eyes. "Do your best. Most dogs don't start to perk up for a few days." He gave a pointed look at the propeller tail and Rocco's bright eyes. "But I think this one will prove me wrong."

"He's got energy," I agreed.

Dr. Johnson touched my arm. "Speaking of energy, are you okay? You look a little"—he hesitated like he realized he was hovering in dangerous territory—"overwhelmed."

"I'm fine."

"Rocco will make a full recovery."

I nodded. "I know."

"Any other questions or concerns?"

Silence descended, and I struggled to hold everything inside. I wasn't the vent-to-strangers type, but there was something about the white coat and doctor's office setting that made me want to spill my guts.

In the end, old patterns persisted and my guts stayed firmly *not* spilled.

I thanked the vet, bent to lift Rocco up—

"It's not your fault," Dr. Johnson said.

My laugh was brittle. "That's what everyone keeps saying."

He raised a brow. "Then it's probably true."

"You're probably right."

A smile and a flirtatious wink. It would have been overkill on a less attractive man. On Dr. Johnson—young and muscular and sweet—it only added to the general appeal.

When had I started to notice the general appeal of other men?

Right around the time that my husband might have been unfaithful.

Any amusement I felt dried up at that thought. Dr. Johnson must have noticed it because he snagged my keys from the exam table, scooped up Rocco, and headed for the door.

"I'll get him settled in your car if you want to head to the checkout desk."

"Thanks," I said, but he was already out the door.

Well, what was seeing one more male's back? They were familiar territory these days.

Sighing, I grabbed my purse and left the exam room.

I paid, careful to save the receipt because Bow Wow Patrol was going to reimburse me, and walked outside to my car. Then stopped dead. Rob was standing next to Dr. Johnson, the pair in an intense conversation.

A conversation that abruptly ended when I came over to them.

Rob gave Dr. Johnson a hard look as he patted Rocco on the head. That look transformed into a fierce glare when the vet stopped in front of me and squeezed my hand.

"Hang in there, okay?" Dr. Johnson waited until I tore my eyes from my husband and met his. "And you need anything, don't hesitate to call." He handed me a card. "Cell's on the back."

"Thank you," I whispered as he walked away.

My gaze hit the pavement, tracing the cracks as I took a deep breath and prepared to navigate the glacial ice storm that was my husband.

Peace. All I wanted was peace.

I shored up my spine. "Hi."

"Hey."

"I—I'm sorry about Rocco. It was a horrible accident, but Dr. Johnson says he'll make a full recovery."

I paused. Waited.

Nothing.

I bit my lip, pressed on. "So, anyway. I need to get him home so he can rest." I hesitated a beat, thinking my husband would respond to me. When he didn't, I went on rambling, "Then I have to pick up Allie and take her to Kelly's for her riding lessons, and for some reason I agreed to ride with them. Then Max has a play-date with Caleb after school then I'll pick him up from soccer and . . ."

I ran out of steam.

And got silence back.

Awesome.

Seriously, why did I bother?

I pushed past my husband. A man who, just months before, I would have said that I knew better than myself.

This cold person in front of me was a stranger.

"I'm tired of being shut out," I muttered, tearing open the passenger door and tossing my purse inside. "I'm tired of feeling like a pathetic puppy that keeps getting kicked. I'm"—I sighed as fatigue flooded through me—"just tired."

Rob was still standing by the open trunk of my van, but now he was scratching Rocco under the chin.

"You shouldn't leave him unsupervised with the trunk open,"

Rob said. "He already got hurt once on your watch. You need to be more careful."

"You mean be more careful and supervise when you're *right* there?" I asked, slamming the door and walking toward the trunk. "Because by my count you've got two eyes and hands, and you're fully capable of supervising."

Rob's stare snapped to mine, but he didn't apologize.

He didn't say anything further either. Which, really, at that point, I considered a win.

I shoved between him and the car, checking that Rocco was safely away from the trunk so I could close it.

"What's this?" Rob asked, fingers plucking into my back pocket.

"What's what?" I asked, after the lift-gate clicked closed.

"This."

I turned, saw that he was holding the card Dr. Johnson had handed me. "It's the vet's card." I shrugged. "He's been very kind and helpful about Rocco."

Rob snorted. "I bet he has."

Are. You. Fucking. Kidding. Me?

Now, I don't get mad often. I really don't. Sure, little things annoy me and pester my thoughts. But I'm the stewing type, not the blow-my-top-like-a-volcano type.

Until I hit the Point.

I'm guessing anyone in the universe could see that I'd hit *that* Point.

Everyone except my husband.

Because he had the flipping audacity to take a step toward me, pin me between the van and his hard body, and glare down at me.

"What's between you and the vet?"

I lost it.

"What's between you and the girl on your phone?" I hissed and shoved at his chest, knocking him back a step. "What's with you and the lipstick on your collar? What's with you and not coming home last night?"

I yelled the last at the top of my lungs.

Pulling air through my nose, I tried to drop the volume of my voice. "I don't know what's going on with you or work or us, but I do know that the last freaking thing you should be spending any energy on is wondering whether or not there is anything between Dr. Johnson and myself. I don't even know the man's first name."

Rob stared at me for a long moment before throwing the card in my face. "It's Sam, and it's right there next to his cell number."

"Great." I crumpled the card in my palm and turned away. The door handle was cool beneath my fingers as I yanked it open.

I threw myself into the seat, tossed the card into the cup holder with a plethora of other trash, and tried to close the door. Unfortunately, it wouldn't go anywhere when I tried to slam it.

"Where are you going?" Rob snapped, his hand holding it open.

"I think I told you that already." I pulled on the door again. It didn't budge. Damn strong fingers.

"I'm not done discussing this," he said.

Ignoring his words and the open door for the time being, I jammed my keys into the ignition and turned on the van. It was a cool day outside, but the interior was getting warm already, so I directed cold air back toward Rocco.

Then I plunked my head on the steering wheel and counted to ten.

When I was done, I lifted my eyes to Rob's. "Why do you have an extra cell phone with someone named Celeste texting you all the time?"

His jaw tightened, but he didn't respond.

"No words now?" I asked. "Or no explanation as to why I'm getting butt dials and overhearing you say I don't matter? That only our kids do?"

"Melissa, it's—"

Hope bubbled up inside me.

"Is this something with work?" I asked desperately when he

hesitated. "Something you can't discuss? Something that isn't about us?"

Please let that be the case.

"You don't have to confirm or deny it," I said, knowing that my words were rushing together as I grasped at any explanation for why my marriage was exploding. "Just wink or something. Or —I've got it! A code word. Marshmallow. Or banana. How about banana?"

Rob shook his head. "It's not work."

Those pretty little bubbles of positivity disintegrated. A giant boulder dropped straight onto my gut.

I was going to be sick.

"It's not work?" I repeated dumbly.

"No."

Breathe. In. Out. *Don't lose it.* "I need to get Allie from school."

"Okay." He dropped his hand from the door, turned away from me.

"Rob?"

He stopped, turned back.

"Don't come home tonight."

16

I wanted to do something reckless.

Dumb and stupid and reckless.

But that wasn't me. So I was here.

Here being on top of a horse under the watchful eye of my sister and staring down at the ground that suddenly seemed like a lot farther than six feet away.

Allie sat on a pony—I was trying not to make a stink that it was several feet shorter than my own horse because she was my daughter, after all—next to me. She was grinning and wriggling in the saddle, beyond excited that I was riding with her.

Kelly was the horse whisperer, not me. I could barely keep my seat and was petrified the entire time.

My daughter, on the other hand, had inherited the horse gene and had quickly moved from corral rides to long, traipsing gallops through the fields of Kel and Justin's ranch.

Roosevelt Ranch was rapidly becoming known as one of the premier horse breeders in the country, and it was all because of my sister. She'd worked with the previous owner of the ranch for years, had even been given a college scholarship because she'd been such a talented equestrian. But when Justin's brother—one Rex Roosevelt and once a serious scumbag—had bought the ranch and nearly driven it into the ground, Justin and Kelly had taken over.

Now it was awesome, and the stables were busy. Which was just the way Kel preferred.

Breeding, boarding, teaching kids—and sometimes adults, in my case—to ride, was what my sister had always dreamed about.

That and a big family.

I smiled as she brought her horse up next to Allie's and adjusted her helmet, tightening the buckle so that it didn't slip from her head. Justin held Abby in his arms and was carrying her through the stables as they checked out the horses.

I had the feeling that Abby would be riding better than me in no time.

"Ready?" Kel asked, coming alongside my horse.

"Did you have to give me the biggest one?" I moaned.

"Yup." A quick smile. "Plus, he's the sweetest one. Theodore—"

"Theodore?" I squawked, ready to launch myself from the saddle. Theodore was known in the stables as the most rambunctious and troublesome of the horses.

"Kidding," Kel said, grabbing my shoulder to steady me. "This is Sweetheart. She's gentle and as sweet as her name. It's where Allie started. We use her for the five-year-olds."

I gripped the reigns tightly. "I hear the amusement in your voice, and I don't like it."

"You'll be fine."

"How'd your doctor's appointment go?" With all of the craziness of the day before, I hadn't thought to ask.

Kel glanced over and whispered out of the side of her mouth. "Twins."

My eyes went wide.

She laughed. "I know. I guess it's not a surprise considering that Justin and Rex are twins, but holy sh"—she cut the word off when Allie glanced over—"horses hooves, three under four. How are we going to survive?"

I forgot that I was on top of an animal-powered death machine for a second and squeezed Kelly's hand. "You'll survive. You're an amazing mom. And Rob—"

The words stalled. I'd been about to say that Rob and I would be there for her.

But would he?

"We'll be there for you guys," I finished, feigning a look down as though Sweetheart had been responsible for the bump in my words. Never mind that she was acting the perfect *sweetheart* and had hardly moved.

Kel, at least, didn't seem to register the blip as anything major. She laughed, repositioned my hands on the reins, and nodded at the rolling hills. "Let's get you moving before you chicken out."

I mock-frowned, shoved the turmoil far, far down. This was my time with Allie and Kelly, and I wasn't going to ruin that.

———

"THAT WAS SO FUN, MOMMY!" Allie yelled as we got back into the car and headed to the field where Max's soccer practice was being held.

We were both dusty and I, for one, was going to be sore in the morning. I'd also agreed for some reason to take more lessons from my sister.

Kelly was convinced that I was going to become an expert horsewoman.

I had my doubts about that.

But it *had* been fun, and so I was coming back in two days for another ride on Sweetheart.

Now that statement sounded both extremely odd and strangely dirty.

"It *was* fun," I told Allie. "Thank you for letting me come with you."

"I love Bruce," she said of her pony. "He's funny."

I grinned back at her in the rearview. "You mean that he poops a lot."

She giggled. "You said poop."

"It's true."

Her laugh warmed me from the inside out. "I love you, Mommy."

"I love you too, Allie-girl."

She broke into a story about a ball, the playground, and two mean girls. Then transitioned into one about the book they'd read at circle time, before discussing the proper piece placement for the doll puzzle at school.

By the time we reached the field, her school stories had run out and she'd moved onto horse ones.

Max ran up to the car, bag hanging on his shoulder. I waved at Caleb's mom, rolling down the window to confirm that I had the boys for the same routine but at our house the following week, then drove home.

Then it was dinner and homework, baths and bedtime reading. By the time I sat down to work on my next blog post it was after ten. I hadn't gotten a bath yet, but I had work to do, lunches to make, and dinner to think about for the following night, since Allie had a late swimming class.

Deciding to combine two tasks into one, I started making the kids' lunches and documented the process for the blog.

Sandwiches and fruit weren't the most exciting blog material, but they were something, and my white cheddar with apricot jelly and sliced green apples on thick crusty pieces of sourdough were to die for.

The combination was one of my favorite snacks, and as thus, I'd just sat down to one on the couch—midnight snacks were the best—when my cell phone buzzed.

"Hello?" I said hesitantly into it when I didn't recognize the number.

"Melissa? It's Tammy."

I somehow both tensed and relaxed at the same time. Tensed

because Tammy held my dreams in the palm of her hand and relaxed because I liked her. A lot.

"H-hi, Tammy. How are you?"

"It's not too late to call, is it?" she asked. "I'd normally never phone this late, but then I got confirmation from the network and got excited, and . . . well, here we are."

I waited until she paused then said, "No. I'm normally up pretty late."

"Oh good. Okay, here's what's going to happen. I've got a flight in two days for you to New York. You'll come out and film a segment in the studio and we'll go from there." I could almost picture her ticking items off on her fingers. "I need two recipes from you by tomorrow so I can have the food purchased."

"Oh, wow. Okay."

"Any recipe you want," Tammy said. "Oh! And I know you need to be home with your kiddos, so I've scheduled you to fly in on a red-eye, film in the morning, and then fly home that same evening." Her voice lowered conspiratorially. "And my hope is that if everything goes well, we can film in your kitchen or your backyard. Ooh! Or maybe we can convince your sister and her yummy of a husband to let us film on the ranch. That would be a gorgeous location. Rolling hills, sweeping sunsets." She sighed. "That kitchen."

I set my plate on the coffee table and sat forward on the couch, my mind spinning.

"Sound good?"

I blinked. "Uh . . ." I hesitated, but only for a split second before I got my stuff together. "Yes. It sounds great."

Already my brain was working on our schedule. Mentally calculating the kids' after-school activities and sorting out the coverage I needed. I had enough food in the freezer for dinner, and I could make breakfast and lunch ahead of time. I'd need to get them to and from school—

"Perfect! I'll email you the details and see you in two days!" Tammy paused. "Don't forget those recipes!"

With a *click*, she hung up, and I stayed put on the couch for a couple of seconds, stunned motionless by the whirlwind that was Tammy.

Then I jumped into motion.

I practically dove into the kitchen, gathering my two favorite recipes: chicken and dumplings and a cabbage-apple slaw.

They were simple, delicious, and easy to make with cheap ingredients.

They were me. They were my blog.

I could stretch several elements to last many meals. And I'd had to on multiple occasions when my mother had gotten drunk and gambled all our money away.

Food had been my demon growing up. Never enough of it, constantly slipping more to Kelly since she was younger, and it was my job to take care of her, to make sure her belly didn't rumble with hunger.

It had gotten so bad that I'd felt guilty for eating, for taking one bite out of her mouth. I'd gotten really skinny. *Too* skinny. Not quite anorexic. At least, I don't think so. But I hadn't been in a healthy mental space.

Rob had saved me from that. And the town.

Darlington was good people. We'd had anonymous deliveries of meals and groceries, from those who knew my mother wasn't a good person. Not that our father was innocent or much better—as an absentee dad, he was just as negligent.

We'd never had any authority intervene on our behalf because I had hidden our problems. Because I hadn't asked for help. Because I'd been scared we would be split up if someone reported us to child protection services.

So when I'd finally gotten a job and could support myself and Kel, I'd pinched every penny and bought cookbooks, studied up with Henry's dad at his restaurant in between waitressing shifts, practiced and experimented and *ate*.

Now food was my therapy.

And I was ready to share it with the world.

I slipped on an apron, pulled out the ingredients. I would run through the recipes, make sure they were perfect.

My phone buzzed, and I extracted it from my pocket. A text from Rob was on the screen.

Go to sleep. It's late.

I gasped, and my eyes flew to the window. Headlights flashed in the driveway before a car backed out and drove away.

I'm going to New York.

Silence then another buzz.

I wish you wouldn't.

I didn't reply. Instead, I rolled out the dough for the dumplings and whipped up the two recipes.

The little balls of dough turned out perfect. Delicious, well-seasoned, and melt-in-your-mouth. The apple slaw was the perfect complement. It was light and tart and contrasted with the creamy sauce nicely.

I stuffed my face, froze the leftovers, only wishing a little bit that Rob was there to sample with me.

I didn't understand what was happening with us, what I'd done wrong.

But I did know that I wasn't giving up on my dream, whether or not my husband wanted me to.

17

"*A*nd I don't know if Rob will be working or not," I said, gathering up my purse and prepping the lie I'd already thought up ahead of time. "He's pretty busy with a big case."

Kelly studied my face for a long moment before nodding and reaching across the console to give me a hug. "Well, Justin and I will be there with Abby so either way. It'll be a big sleepover."

I winked. "I don't think you'll be getting a lot of sleep."

Justin was with the kids, and they'd been running around the backyard like maniacs when Kel and I had driven away two hours before.

"I'm considering this training for what's to come," she said.

I cupped her cheeks in my palms. "I love you."

"That's because I'm awesome." She nudged me in the direction of the terminal. "Now, go. I'll try not to burn dinner tomorrow."

"How about you try not to burn *anything*?" I laughed, shook my head at her extended middle finger, and got out of the car. My suitcase was in the trunk so I retrieved it and with a wave to my sister, threw my purse over my shoulder, and headed inside.

I was flying out of the Salt Lake City airport, and it felt strange to be by myself. Strange in that it was *easy*.

I walked to the counter, waited in line, and checked my suitcase without once having to referee a fight or tell someone to keep their voice down. It was so quiet.

And honestly, I was torn between really liking it and feeling a little lonely.

My kids were awesome. I loved them to Jupiter and back.

Yes, they could drive me up a wall. Yes, it was nice to have quiet. But I also missed hanging out with them.

Not having them next to me made me realize just how isolating my life had become over the last few years.

I needed to make an effort to get out more, to reconnect with old friends. I'd been trailing in the wake of my life for so long, just trying to get through, just barely surviving the homework and after-school activities, Rob's constantly changing hours, and the blog.

And what was the result?

I was lonely.

I had my kids. I had my sister and her family. But my life felt a little empty.

Well, that was going to change.

I was going to change.

———

I woke, eyes crusty and mind groggy at a voice blaring through speakers.

". . . the plane is preparing for descent, please place your tray tables and seat backs in the upright position."

Blinking, I shifted, stretching my sore neck and thinking it had been a lot easier to sleep on a plane when I'd been younger.

Though I'd only flown two times before—to my honeymoon with Rob and back.

Those times I'd had a warm chest to cuddle into, strong arms to keep me upright.

A flash of memory sparked to life in my mind. Crystal blue

water and white sand. Hot, sticky air. Jerk chicken. Plantains. More spice than I'd ever experienced in my life.

And Rob.

Rob smiling down at me. Rob holding me close on the ocean's edge, the bright orange sun fading into the horizon. Rob with eyes that softened as he looked at me.

The jar of the plane bumping against the tarmac pulled me out of my reverie.

Then came the taxiing to the gate, the long wait as the doors were opened and people filed off. I shuffled my way up the aisle like the rest of the cattle.

The airport air was stale. I wrinkled my nose as I made my way through the terminal and toward baggage claim.

Please let my knives have arrived in one piece.

I was wrinkled, my clothes rumpled and my hair no doubt sticking up in multiple directions. I needed a shower, a good bed, and about two days straight of sleep.

But since that wasn't on the docket, I slipped into a bathroom, pulled out my makeup bag, and made the best of it. I brushed teeth and hair, fixed smudged eyeliner, and added lip gloss.

Taking a big breath, I focused on my reflection in the mirror, encouraging the fierceness in my pale brown eyes. I nodded once in approval, shoved my makeup bag into my purse, and marched toward baggage claim.

I had this.

————

I SO DID NOT HAVE this.

I was ridiculously incompetent: fumbling with my knives, calling ingredients by the wrong names, and forgetting to wash my hands after handling raw chicken.

So freaking stupid.

I could do these recipes with my eyes closed, but I couldn't apparently do them with the black, unfeeling eye of the camera fixed on me.

"I'm sorry," I said as Tammy came over. "I'm nervous. I know I need to get it together."

She smiled, but her gaze held concern. "Don't worry. Nerves are totally normal."

What was not normal, I was sure, was the amount of bungling I was accomplishing.

Stupid. So stupid. I was going to ruin my marriage and this opportunity in one shot.

"Why don't you step outside and take a quick break? Call home, zone out for ten minutes. I'm going to have the studio cleaned up, and we'll start again for a few more takes."

I nodded and wiped my—now clean—hands on a towel. "Okay. Thanks."

The studio I was in was on the third floor of a building somewhere in New York City. I said somewhere because I literally had no clue where I was, other than surrounded by skyscrapers, traffic, and chilled air tinged with the stink of too many cars and people.

New York was some people's mojo, but it definitely wasn't mine.

A car had picked me up from the airport and driven me straight to the studios, where I'd met several executives. *That* part had gone well. They were friendly and we'd had a good rapport.

Then had come the camera.

Staring at me.

I shuddered and pulled out my phone to call Kel.

At the last moment, I changed and called Rob.

I don't know if it was because I was alone and he'd always been my rock. I don't know if I was glutton for punishment. I don't know if I just missed my husband and wanted any piece of him that he was willing to give.

Ring.

Ring.

Ring.

Ring.

My heart clenched hard. I needed him and he wasn't there. Again—

"Hello?"

My words caught in my throat, stifling my response.

"Miss? You there?"

For some idiotic reason, I nodded, though he couldn't see me, and the lack of my answer made frustration radiate through the airwaves.

He sighed, and I heard a rustle, knew he was about to hang up.

"Rob," I whispered, thinking it was too late, that it was too quiet, that he was already gone.

"Melissa."

It was just my name in his voice, but it meant so much more. "Hey," I said. "I just—"

"Needed me."

My nerves slipped, the sadness slid away. Irritation flooded in instead.

"I don't—"

"Melissa. I talked with Justin when I came home last night and Kelly was driving you to the airport." His voice went a little harder. "Thanks for letting me know about the trip, by the way."

"I told you I was going. Plus when were we supposed to chat?" I interjected. "You haven't exactly—"

He ignored me. "I'm assuming you've arrived in New York and you're second-guessing yourself. Every time that you do something out of your comfort zone you do this."

"I—"

"You're good enough, Miss. Trust that."

I paused, letting the words wash over me, holding them close.

"If that's it, then I need to go."

I pursed my lips together. Throwing me a tiny bone, then right back to normal.

At least I knew where I stood.

"Thanks for the pep talk. It was—" I shook my head. "You did your duty. I won't bug you again."

"Melis—"

Pressing that red circle felt good.

I turned my phone to silent when it rang again and stared at the lock screen as I rejected the call. Allie and Max had their arms around each other and were giggling like fools.

This is why I was here. So they could see me as enough. Not just their mom, not just a robot to clean up after them, a short order cook to make their meals.

I had value and—I closed my eyes, took a long inhale, and let it out slowly—I wanted them to see it.

I wanted Rob to see it.

I—

"Ready?"

Tammy smiled at me from the open doorway.

Slipping my phone into my pocket, I smiled back. "I'm ready."

18

"That was fantastic," Tammy said, clapping her hands together.

I breathed a mental sigh of relief and set down the plate I was holding. "Once I got over the camera."

"That's the hardest part," she agreed and came forward, hugging me tight as she whispered in my ear, "Nothing's set in stone, of course. But this is going to knock everyone's socks off."

I pulled back slightly, taking in her kind blue eyes, porcelain skin, and curly red hair. She was beautiful in an Irish nymph sort of way. "You think?"

A nod. "I know."

My knees felt a little weak, but it was from joy and relief, rather than fear for a change.

"Well, phew."

She laughed and slipped her arm around my waist. "Now come on, we have time for an early dinner before I have to get you back to the airport."

"That sounds perfect," I said.

New York wasn't so bad, I thought an hour later, eyeing the gorgeous plate in front of me and not wanting to ruin its beauty by sticking my fork in it.

"Pork belly with caramelized walnuts, a cranberry vinaigrette, and micro greens," the server said.

"Aka very tasty bacon," Tammy said with a wink.

"This looks incredible." The pork belly was a gorgeous brown, and when topped with the crimson-colored dressing and edible flowers, the whole effect was stunning.

"If you keep looking at it, it'll just get cold," Tammy whispered.

"True," I said with a grin and dug in.

Then promptly moaned.

So, *so* good.

"Okay," I said once I'd finished the entire portion, stopping just short of licking the plate. "New York may not have the wide open skies and fresh air of Utah, but it's not the worst."

"If you love food, there's no better place," Tammy said.

At that moment, as a plate with a gorgeous chocolate tart was being set down in front of me, I found I couldn't disagree.

———

"MOM!" Justin and I walked through the door to find the kids sitting at the round table. Kel was perched on the countertop, eyeing the coffee pot like it was a pile of gold and she was a marauding pirate.

"Have a cup," I told her as the kids jumped up from the table and hugged me tightly. Their little arms could squeeze hard when they were motivated. I squeezed back. "Missed you little munchkins."

"I already had one," my sister said with a pouty lip.

Justin scooped up Abby and wrapped his free arm around Kel's waist. "Decaf?" he offered.

My sister frowned. "What's the point?"

"The taste?" Justin said.

"If there's no caffeine, there's no point," Kelly declared. "I'd rather have my calories in chocolate. Or—oh!" Her eyes found mine as I stood and the kids ran back to the table to finish their breakfast. "Can you make that blueberry pie again? With the fresh whipped cream? And the crumbly crust?"

I laughed. "Sure. Let me get the kids off to school, and I'll whip one up."

"Oh," Kel's eyes flicked over my shoulder. "I thought Rob was taking them."

"Rob's at work—" I turned, words stopping when I saw my husband standing in the doorway behind me.

"Can Daddy drive us, Mom?" Max asked.

Traitor.

But I smiled and nodded, not looking at Rob as I crossed to the fridge and pulled open the door. "Of course."

I didn't miss the look Kel and Justin exchanged as an awkward silence fell over the kitchen. A silence that was broken when Allie spilled her glass of milk all over the table and floor.

Perfect. A distraction was just what I needed.

I snatched up a towel and a bottle of cleaner, reassuring Allie when she would have started crying that it was just an accident and not a big deal. I bustled around, mopping up the milk, pouring another glass for Allie, grabbing a pack of cinnamon rolls out of the freezer and shoving them in Kel's hands as I all but pushed her, Justin, and, consequently, Abby out the door.

My sister gave me squinty eyes over her shoulder and I knew a hard conversation was coming soon.

Ugh.

But Rob was behind me, still in the doorway, still quiet and staring. I called goodbye to my sister, Justin, and Abby then whipped up two lunches for the kids and crammed them into their backpacks, which I plunked onto their shoulders.

"Hurry now," I said, "or you'll be late for school."

Hugs and kisses to the kids, swirling around, avoiding my husband, being a busy bee pretending all is perfect.

"You forgot to kiss Dad, Mom," Max said. "You always kiss Dad."

I froze, eyes locking with Rob's.

He leaned in. I bent forward, closed my eyes, and waited.

His lips hit my . . . cheek.

"All right, buddy," Rob said. "Let's hit it before we're late."

I thought I was a strong person, but in that moment I felt very weak.

The kids were out the door. The house was quiet. I was alone and holding a carton of blueberries.

What the hell was I doing with my life?

19

"Hey," a feminine voice said two days later. The greeting was accompanied by red nails scratching lightly down his spine.

Rob shivered, slung an arm around Celeste's waist to tug her tightly against him. She slid closer still, and plunked her ass into his lap. He shifted, adjusting those hourglass curves sideways over his legs.

"Is that a banana in your pocket . . ." she began, lips curved up and one perfectly shaped eyebrow raised.

"No," he muttered, jutting his chin up and flicking his eyes over her shoulder when she glanced back at him.

Her bottom lip slipped out for a moment before she sighed and looked forward.

They were in deep, four towns over where Celeste had stumbled upon a lead for who was dealing in the Tri-Hills. And by deep, Rob meant that he didn't know the next time he would be home. He hadn't been able to tell Melissa or his co-workers about the case.

It had all happened fast. He'd pitched Celeste's plan to his chief and they'd fine-tuned the cover—Rob was out on parole for an arms deal gone bad. Celeste was his girlfriend who liked the white powder too much.

Celeste's source had then secured them a meet . . . or rather an invitation to a party filled with addicts and criminals.

The rest was up to them. They were to infiltrate the group and find the supplier.

And because there was some suspicion that the dealer was being assisted by dirty cops, he and Celeste were strictly reporting to their chief, who was working with the police chief of *this* town on a one-on-one basis.

It was a shit show. A twisted mess and a plan that screamed half-cocked. Alone and one wrong move could mean their lives.

But Rob just had to think about the murdered girl to get his head on straight.

If he didn't solve this, if he didn't manage to remove this poison from the Tri-Hills, Allie could end up the same.

Damaged. Broken. Scared.

Dead.

So for now, they partied. The house was gross, stinking, and disgusting. There was booze, piles of drugs around—lines of coke literally dotted every flat surface in sight—and what he assumed were illegal guns.

He was fucking miserable.

When he'd been promoted to detective, his thoughts had drifted toward stolen pies from the bakery and teenagers releasing goats in high school hallways.

Not drugs and weapons and murdered girls in nondescript warehouses.

Not a woman who wasn't his wife sitting in his lap while he was deep undercover.

Not a wife who seemed intent on frosting him out and choosing her precious recipes over him.

Or a family who didn't seem to miss him when he was gone. He'd left a note because it was early. Had expected a text or call in response before he'd had to lock his personal cell phone away.

Instead, he'd gotten nothing.

Maybe he'd been working too long of hours for too many years. Maybe he'd put other people before his family. Maybe he'd pushed everyone away.

But he couldn't get that young face out of his mind, nameless, lifeless, and so pale. Her body stained with blood and bruises. Her skirt shoved up, fear fixed in the position of her limbs, in the scratches and marks on her arms.

She'd fought.

And he was throwing everything he had into fighting for her too.

Celeste laughed—a shrill, annoying sound that grated on his nerves. But the man sitting across from them seemed to like it. He crooked a finger at her, and Celeste clambered out of his lap, flashing him her red lace thong in the process.

He used to think that ass was gorgeous, but now it just seemed like she was trying too hard.

She dropped herself in the man's lap—tall, expensive suit, clear eyes unlike the rest of the druggies in the room—ran her hand down his chest, and leaned up to whisper in his ear.

The man glanced down at Celeste, studied her for a long minute, then smiled as he trailed fingers up her thigh.

Rob stood, ready to stop the man from assaulting his partner, cover be damned.

Celeste stopped him.

By grabbing the man's hand and tugging it higher.

20

"What do you think about my nails, Auntie Kelly?" Allie lifted her hand and showed off the alternating pattern of purple and bright pink. "Mommy says she's going to put sparkles on too."

I smiled and glanced over at Max and Justin, who were watching some animated show about teenaged superheroes. "Should we do Aunt Kelly's next?" I asked, smiling teasingly at my sister, who was about as far from sparkles and hot pink as a woman can get.

Allie giggled, which made Abby laugh, and Kel raised her hands in surrender.

"Not for me, silly girl. Nail polish doesn't hold up too long in the stables."

Justin glanced over, winked. "But I was looking forward to seeing you sparkle."

I sent him a mock-glare. "You're supposed to say that your wife always sparkles."

"I wasn't sparkling much when I was losing my guts this morning."

I glanced back at my sister. "Oh no. Has it started already?"

She nodded. "Worse than last time." A shrug. "I guess that's to be expected with two of them this time."

Allie cocked her head. "Two of what?"

We all froze before Justin came up with the best distraction for my horse-crazy Allie.

"Horses. Two new ones in the stables."

Allie shrieked. Which made Abby shriek. Which made Max glare and cover his ears.

"Actually, we have three new horses boarding this week." Kel's eyes caught Justin's, and I had difficulty holding back my jealousy at the shared look of understanding that passed between them. Rob and I used—

No.

"One is only two years old," Kel continued. "With the cutest heart-shaped marking just between his eyes."

"Really?" Allie clapped her hands together, probably mussing the polish I'd just painstakingly applied. "Can I come tomorrow and see him? Please? *Please?*"

Kelly laughed. "You know you're welcome any time, but," she added when Allie began spinning in circles and jumping up and down, "you need to check with your mom first."

I glanced down at my phone, frowning when I saw the calendar jam-packed with after-school activities. "Tomorrow isn't going to work, sweetheart."

The bottom lip came out.

God, she was cute. It wasn't going to work, but she was still cute.

"Max has soccer, and we're driving carpool, and you have Girl Scouts right after school." I shook my head. "We just won't have time to get out to the ranch."

"But—"

"We still have our riding lesson the day after, so we'll go over then, okay?"

The bottom lip didn't move.

Then it did, transforming into a brilliant smile.

"Daddy can drive me."

Her dad, whom I'd texted and hadn't gotten any response from. Who'd simply left a note saying:

On a case, not sure when I'll be home.
-R

Was that days? Hours? Weeks? *Months?* For how long?

Her dad. Who'd already been gone for two days, and I was still no closer to answering any of those questions.

"Dad will probably be working," I said. "We can't—"

I cut the words off before I could say "count on him." Because our kids didn't need to hear their father wasn't reliable.

"Dad is never home," Max grumbled.

I didn't affirm that I had been thinking the same thing for a while. Instead I said, "Dad does a very important job. He's helping to keep everyone safe."

My sister made a noise, but when I looked over at her, she wouldn't make eye contact with me.

I frowned.

Max sighed. "I know," he said, his voice wavering the slightest bit. "I just wish that he could make some of my games. I've been working really hard."

Max *had* been practicing hard. He'd been practically living and breathing soccer for weeks.

"Dad will be so impressed at the next game he comes to, buddy," I said. "You've improved so much."

"Yeah."

Max reached for the remote, turned off the TV, and stood. "I'm tired. I'm going to bed." He said goodbye to Justin and Kelly and goodnight to his sister before heading up the stairs.

"I'm tired" were words I'd never heard him utter before.

He was a fighter of sleep, not an acceptor. Always had been.

Which meant he was upset. Certainly about his dad, but what if it was something else as well?

"I—"

"Go," Kelly said. "We need to head home anyway." She scooped up Allie and pulled her in for a hug. "Go brush away those sugar bugs on your teeth, and I'll see if I can pick you up from Girl Scouts tomorrow, deal?"

"Yes!" Allie fist-pumped then sprinted upstairs to her bathroom.

"You don't have—"

"Don't you dare finish that sentence," my sister said. "I've got auntie privileges, and indoctrinating Allie to horses is one of them." Her voice dropped. "But I have sister privileges too, which means we need to talk about what's going on with Rob. Things aren't right between you two."

I sighed and dropped my head forward, staring at the one nice pair of flats that Rocco hadn't managed to destroy—probably since he was still uncomfortable and moving quite slow with the cast and cone of shame.

But staring at the blue leather didn't make the truth any less obvious.

"They're not right," I said. "We're not in a good place."

"Have you . . . well, tried to talk about it?"

My eyes flew up, locked with hers. "All I've done is try to get through to him, but there's nothing there in return. No under-standing, no support! He didn't want me to go to New York. He hates the blog. He hates that I've found something to spend time on that's not devoted solely to him." My chest heaved. "It's—I just don't know what to do. I probably won't even get the show, but how could he begrudge me the chance? This is the one thing I've always wanted . . ."

"I know, Miss."

"Culinary school was too expensive when I had the chance." I leaned back against the wall, rattling the framed pictures of Rob and me and the kids—happy, cuddling, giggling—that lined the hallway. "Then I had to drop out of college to work and pay to put Rob through the academy." My hands were fists, and I smacked one against my thigh. "I did it because I loved him, because I wanted the chance for him to do what he loved. So, after everything we've been through, how could he begrudge me that?"

Abby squawked in Kelly's arms, and I jumped, having completely forgotten that she and Justin were still in the room.

This is why I bottled things up. This is why I didn't vent about the really big stuff to other people and *especially* not to Kel. Once the statements were out there, I couldn't take them back. They were always there, tainting future interactions, influencing how they would relate to Rob.

I didn't want to ruin their relationship with him.

I didn't want to badmouth him to them.

I just . . . wanted my husband back.

Justin's expression was fierce. "I'll pay for you to go to culinary school if you don't get the job." He reached over and pulled me into a hug. "And if you do get the job, you can film at the ranch. I'll get a babysitter to help with the kids." He leaned back. "God knows, we're going to need all hands on deck as it is."

"You don't have to—"

Justin snagged Abby from Kel's arms. "We're here for you, Melissa. We're family, and that means we have your back, Rob be damned." He glanced at Kelly. "I'll get her settled. Come out when you're ready."

He slipped out the front door, closing it quickly behind him and limiting the rush of cold autumn air into the warm house.

Abby's jacket was on the bench by the front door, as well as the diaper bag. I scooped up both and handed them to Kel.

She was looking at me sadly. "Is it really that bad?"

I nodded.

"Damn."

Silence. Then, "I know."

"I thought you guys had it all figured out."

My laugh was brittle. "Believe me, I did too."

She played with the zipper on Abby's purple coat. Pulling it up, down, up, down. "What happened?"

"I wish I could say I knew exactly what." My hands found the hem of my shirt, and I ran my fingers over the threads forming the seam. "He was promoted to detective six months ago, you know, and he's just been different."

"Different how?"

"Distant? I try to talk to him, and he seems unavailable. Longer hours."

"Do you think the job is getting to him?"

"That and—" Oh God, was I seriously going to confide in my sister about this? It was so . . . embarrassing, I guess, that my husband might be cheating on me.

What kind of woman did that make me? What kind of wife?

Kel's hands froze. "What?"

"I think he's having an affair."

21

---

*M*y sister's eyes met mine, and there was a shadow in them.

A shadow that made my stomach drop.

"You know something," I said and, yes, there was accusation in my tone, but she was my sister. And if she knew something but hadn't said—

"I don't know anything." Kelly winced. "Okay, there was a rumor, but that was it. I heard it once and never again." She shrugged, bit her lip. "I just assumed it was small-town gossip at its best."

Damn.

I slumped back against the console table in the hall, the one that Rocco always managed to knock over. Probably because two of the legs were wobbly, I remembered . . . right before I almost went ass over teakettle two feet from the front door.

"Easy," Kel said, in that calming voice of hers. The one that made even the most rambunctious of horses settle. "Everything is—"

"It's not small-town life. Not—" I broke off. "Not after everything I've heard and seen."

Red lipstick on his collar.

She's not important.

My kids are.

"What did you hear? What have you seen?" Steel in that tone now, and while I appreciated the layer of I'm-gonna-cut-a-bitch, there I was again, sharing too much information. Unfairly influencing.

"Anyway," I said. "He hasn't come out explicitly and confirmed anything, but he's not here. He says he's on a case, but he doesn't respond to my messages, doesn't pick up when I call." I sighed, deciding to just let it all come out. The damage was already done. "He has another phone with text messages from a woman named Celeste. Add in bright red lipstick on his collar . . ."

A bright red that didn't match my skin tone, but that wasn't exactly the point now, was it?

"Celeste McDermot?"

My eyes flashed up. "I don't know," I said. "Why?"

"Because last I heard there was a Celeste at the station. A transfer from Denver who was looking to get her teeth into some real case work."

I frowned. "What kind of case work is there in Darlington? Stolen cows? A run-over mailbox?"

Kel shrugged. "I haven't heard anything else. Maybe she was on desk duty or something in Denver and wanted to actually patrol, or something."

"Well, I don't think patrolling involves calling my husband baby, do you?"

"No," Kel said. "It doesn't."

We fell silent.

I opened my mouth, to say what, I really had no idea. I'd felt this way since I saw the first text, as though the foundation of my life had been shaken off its piers.

And I guess that wasn't surprising.

My life and Rob's had been intertwined forever . . . or, well, since grade school.

He'd been there through my mother's various abandonments —when she would take our money and disappear to gamble it away. I'd gotten smarter as time went on, trying to hide the cash I'd earned from odd jobs, from my shifts at the diner in little caches throughout the house.

But she'd always found them.

And when nineteen-year-old Rob had let me hide it at his apartment, tucked in a shoebox under his bed, my mother had cleaned out Kelly's bank account.

Classy, she was.

It had been a while now, thankfully, since I had seen or heard from her. My mother may be dead, for all I knew.

How horrible of a person did that make me for not caring what had happened to her?

I should have compassion for a troubled woman, abandoned by a deadbeat husband, two mouths to feed, and no money.

Except, I remembered.

I remembered her turning the donations away, not caring to accept food for us and only wanting cash. I remembered coming home to find the house torn to shreds because she'd been searching for more money.

I remembered my stomach growling and trying to stretch food so that Kel wouldn't be hungry.

I remembered having to figure out how to pay bills, taking cash directly to the power company and the city offices just so we'd have electricity and water.

I remembered mowing every lawn in our neighborhood, delivering the paper, babysitting, working at the diner.

I remembered it all.

But most of all, the hardest, most piercing memory of that time is me trying every single damned thing I could do to make her love us.

It hadn't worked.

And now, I guess, I had a husband who felt the same way.

Kel hugged me tight. "I love you, you know that, right?"

I sniffed, nodded. "Yup." I forced a laugh. "And you're not so bad yourself."

She pulled back, cupped my cheek. "I need to get out there."

"Go," I said and opened the door. "Take care of them. Don't worry about me."

Kel squeezed my hand as she passed. "Someone has to."

22
———

"*J*ust you and me, kid," I told Rocco a few days later.

His tail thumped in response, bouncing against the couch cushion. I'd had a "no pets on the furniture" policy when we'd first gotten him.

I snorted. Yeah, which had lasted all of a couple of hours.

But on this night, cool air creeping into the house and the heater not making headway on the chill in my bones, I was happy to have the little fluffball of energy next to me.

Even if I'd had to lift him onto the couch.

His leg was healing, but his injuries had definitely taken their toll. He moved a little slower, a little more painfully.

Yay, another thing to feel guilty about.

Dr. Johnson said that he would be stiff and sore for a while, but by the time six weeks rolled around, it would be a challenge to keep him calm. I'd even seen glimpses of that deadly propeller tail and pair of mischievous eyes in the exam room.

But two weeks in, another X-ray to make sure the bones were setting properly, and a fresh, smaller cast, and there was still no sign of his former puppy exuberance. He was more careful, more guarded, and less of an innocent goof.

"So rom-com or action?" I asked, picking up the remote and scanning through the movies available for free.

Allie and Max were having a sleepover at Kelly and Justin's. They were watching the latest kids' flick, not even out in theaters yet, since Justin apparently knew someone in Hollywood who was a big-time producer.

Food TV and Hollywood. Kel had jumped a few degrees in social circles when she'd married Justin.

Not that anyone would know if they ever met him outside of the office. He wore T-shirts and cargo pants.

Cargo pants.

With like a hundred and seventy pockets.

As a former military medic, he said he needed to be prepared, but I rather thought that his affinity for cargo pants was like women with dresses that had pockets.

I love your dress.

Thanks! It has pockets!

Snorting, I made my selection. "Romance," I announced to Rocco.

His tail thumped again.

"Glad you agree."

He sighed.

"Always a critic," I muttered. And now I was having a conversation with a dog. Great.

Still, I scratched his head, settled back with some sea salt and garlic butter popcorn, and lost myself in the movie.

The boy and girl met, fell in love before the girl messed up, causing the boy to leave, and they'd just about gotten back together before my eyes got too heavy and I drifted off.

I woke sometime later, the house dark and cold, Rocco snoring next to me.

I couldn't tell what had woken me. A creak? A buzz? I glanced at my phone and the screen was blank of notifications. All I saw was the picture of the four of us—Rob, Allie, Max, and me—acting crazy and covered in white after a flour fight while making some pie. Kel had taken the picture, and I'd always loved how happy and carefree we'd been in that moment.

But the picture wasn't why I was awake.

Creak.

That wasn't the house settling, that was the loose board in the hallway.

Rocco was suddenly awake, his hackles coming up, a deep growl resonating out of his chest before he burst from the couch and took off down the hall.

His reaction finally made me move. I unlocked my phone, dialed 9-1-1, and found the nearest weapon.

Never more had I wished for a gun in the house, but aside from Rob's service weapon, I didn't normally like having any firearms at home.

Rocco's nails scratched against the floor, his cast making a scraping noise as he turned the corner. I heard a male grunt and a crash before Rocco made a high-pitched squeal of pain.

My heart dropped, and I clutched the lamp tighter as dispatch picked up.

I rattled off my address. "Someone has broken into my house. They're still here—" Rocco gave a ferocious bark before crying out again. Shit. Shit. "Hurry!"

Then I did what was probably—no, was *certainly*—a really stupid thing. I hung up the phone and took off into the hallway, lamp raised.

But all I saw was the front door slamming closed.

I flicked on the lights, swiveled around behind me, afraid someone was going to sneak behind me, like in the movies.

The house was still. Quiet.

Rocco whined.

"Oh, honey," I said, tears stinging my eyes. "You did so good, buddy." I crouched and set the lamp down, seeing his crumpled form and the pain shading his black eyes. "I'm so sorry."

I needed to move him. I was scared to hurt him more than the man had already done, but he was right in the path of the door and shards of glass were all around. Wincing when one bit into the bottom of my bare foot, I carefully slid my arms under his body and lifted.

He whined.

"It's okay, honey. It's okay." I moved as gently as I could, hardly noticing the pain in my feet as more glass sliced through my skin.

I was just setting him on the couch when I heard the sirens and screeching tires as the—two, by the sound of it—cruisers pulled into my driveway.

"Police!" they shouted through the front door.

Rocco growled.

"It's okay," I told him. "I'm here!" I yelled. "In the family room."

The front door banged open, and footsteps pounded down the hall.

One of the officers—McMann, I thought his name was—came into the room, while several of the others fanned out to presumably search the house.

"I think he's gone," I said.

McMann nodded. "We'll check anyway."

"Okay," I said.

We waited in silence for a few minutes. Finally footsteps came down the stairs, and a gruff voice declared. "All clear."

I glanced away from Rocco and saw McMann, two officers I didn't know by name, and Hayden, one of Rob's close friends and a regular visitor to our house.

Or used to be. Before he'd gotten married and found a wife who was able to keep the self-professed worst-chef-in-Darlington in edible food.

"Melissa, are you okay?" he asked, crouching down in front of me.

"I'm fine," I said. "I know you have to question me, but can I please call Dr. Johnson first? I'm worried about Rocco and—"

My voice broke, but I took a breath and forced it to steady out.

"I want him to be seen as soon as possible."

"Of course," Hayden said. "Where are the kids?"

"Kel's," I said.

He released a sigh of relief. "Good night for it."

I nodded and stood. Then nearly collapsed back down with the first step.

Now that I'd noticed it, my feet burned horribly. I glanced down and saw blood staining the carpet.

"You're hurt," Hayden said, reaching to steady me.

"Just a few cuts from the glass," I said, limping toward the kitchen. "I'd forgotten."

"Wait—"

I didn't. I knew Dr. Johnson's card was somewhere, and he'd written his cell on it. I'd taken it from the car and put it with a stack of papers that I needed to sort through but never seemed to find the time. The vet office would be closed, so I needed his cell number.

"Miss, stop," Hayden began. "You're getting blood all over—"

"Doesn't matter," I said, rifling through the stack and sighing with relief when I saw the card near the top.

"Find what you're looking for?"

I nodded, held up the card.

"Good." Hayden swept me off my feet, nodded at McMann. "Call an ambulance." I started to protest the last, but he cut me off as he set me gently on the couch. "Your feet are sliced to ribbons," he gritted out. "Now sit and don't move. I'll grab your cell."

Rocco eyed Hayden a little warily but didn't growl again. He seemed to realize that the officers were the good guys, there to help.

Or maybe he recognized their uniforms because Rob used to wear one so often.

Hayden handed me the phone then crossed back over to McMann and the others. They began to discuss perimeters, patrols, and paperwork as I dialed Dr. Johnson's number.

It rang a few times before a groggy voice answered. "Hello?"

"Hi, uh, Dr. Johnson. This is Melissa, Rocco's—" My voice caught.

I heard rustling on the other end. "What's wrong?"

"Someone broke in, Rocco tried to protect me. He's hurt really bad, can I bring him in?"

"Are you safe?" His voice was fierce.

"The police are here," I said. "I'm good."

"I'm coming over."

"I can—"

"I'll see you in five minutes."

"Okay, the address is—"

"This is Darlington, Melissa. I know where you live." And he hung up.

When I set the phone down, Hayden glanced up from his conversation with McMann and came over. "There's a delay in the ambulance. They're stuck on a couple of calls in Campbell. Apparently tonight's a busy night. We'll drive you to the hospital."

"Dr. Johnson will be here in a few minutes. Rocco—"

He nodded. "We'll wait, and in the meantime, Davis and Cranz are going to go grab some plywood to board up your front door. They broke the sidelight to get in."

Ah. That's why there had been so much glass. Our front door only had one small window, but next to it was one of those long, skinny panes of glass. It had always been convenient to see who was at the door—read, avoid solicitors. Although, I supposed the pane also made it easy to see *inside* . . . and created a boatload of glass shards when someone decided to break in.

"I need to sweep up—"

"McMann is on it."

My bottom lip trembled, and so I bit it. Hard.

"None of that," Hayden said, but his voice was gentle. "You're one of us. We look after our own."

23

I winced as the nurse sprayed something cold and antiseptic into the cuts on my feet.

"Sorry," she said.

"I'm fine." But tears burned, and I bit my bottom lip to keep from crying out.

"Just a bit more glass," the nurse said and probed, probably gently but it felt like the fires of hell. "Almost done."

"Uh-huh," I said through gritted teeth.

"You know that my sister's daughter is in Allie's class. Ashley is my niece." She stopped, glanced up at me.

"Ashley's great," I felt obliged to reply. She *was* great, but while the nurse was clearly trying to distract me, I couldn't help but think this was really not the time for small talk.

She glanced back down. "My name is Haley, and my sister is—"

"Maggie," I said.

"Right." Another squirt of burning cold. How a liquid could set my skin on fire with sensation and yet still feel icy was beyond me. "She gave me a piece of that banana cream pie you made when she had Luke, and it was seriously the best thing I've ever eaten."

Food.

Now *that* was something that could take my mind off things.

"I love that recipe." I sighed. "The whipped cream. The fresh banana flavor." Haley switched feet, but I barely noticed. "There's nothing medicinal about it. And it's so rich. Perfect for a mom who needs a little indulgence after a baby."

"Plus, she said it freezes well," Haley added.

"It does," I said, excited now. "And you can add chocolate chips and a ganache and it's extra decadent."

"What else do you like to cook?"

I laughed. "What *don't* I like to cook, I think is a better question." Haley smiled up at me. "I like recipes that are simple and fresh for the most part, but I don't mind getting lost in something that occasionally needs careful balancing of a bunch of items in my pantry. It's like an extra difficult Sudoku or something."

Haley snorted. "Well, I admire you. I can't cook a thing to save my life."

"Come over," I offered spontaneously before frowning. "When I have a front door again, that is. I'll show you a few things."

"Really?" She set the tweezers on the tray and picked up the dreaded squirt bottle again.

"Really," I said through gritted teeth.

"Cool." A pause. "Last time, I promise."

I nodded as she let loose a stream from the bottle, mentally cursing up a storm even as I tried to distract myself from the pain by recounting substitutes for sugar in my favorite cake recipes.

"Done," she said. "The doctor will probably glue some of the smaller wounds, but a few will need stitches."

I wrinkled my nose.

"I know." She stood and started rummaging through cupboards, setting out various supplies as a familiar face walked into the exam room.

"Dr. Johnson," I said, surprised.

He smiled. "I won't stay long, but I just wanted to come and tell you in person that Rocco is fine. A little banged and bruised, but no internal injuries and his leg is still healing correctly."

I swallowed hard. "Thank you."

His hand found mine and gripped tight. He leaned close. "Where's your husband?"

I shrugged. "Working."

But I think the uncertainty must have shown in my tone because his eyes held mine for a long moment.

I didn't blink, *couldn't* blink. There was an intensity in Dr. Johnson's gaze that made my pulse speed up. It reminded me of the way Rob had looked at me. The way he *used* to look at me.

I wanted that. So badly.

Unfortunately, I didn't want it from this man.

"Dr. Johnson," I began.

"Sam."

"Sam," I repeated. "I can't—"

His lips quirked into a rueful smile. "I know."

The doctor—the people one, rather than the animal one—popped into the room and began peppering me and Haley with questions.

We both answered with alacrity until he sat on a rolling stool and started demanding supplies while engaging Dr. Johnson —*Sam*—in conversation about his practice.

Haley glanced up at me and rolled her eyes.

I rolled them back, at least until the shot came.

If I'd thought the irrigation that Haley had done had hurt, the shot numbing the bottom of each foot was way worse.

"It's better if you don't look," Sam said, turning my face toward his. He dropped his voice to a whisper. "Also, that guy is an arrogant jerk, but he's the best plastic surgeon for miles."

"How do you know that?"

"Because Justin called in a few favors to get him here," he murmured, warm breath hitting my ear.

It was a strangely intimate place to be, wrapped in a pair of arms that weren't my husband's.

"Which I know," he continued, "because I called Justin myself."

I stiffened, and this time not from the shot. My feet were numb, the only sensation I could feel now a distant tugging.

Which was unnerving, but also not the point.

I pulled back, glared.

"Your sister needed to know."

"I know," I said. "But not until morning. She's—she needs her rest."

Sam raised a brow. "I *know*," he replied, saying he knew clearly why my sister needed rest. There really were no secrets in Darlington. "Which is why I called Justin instead. He needed to be aware in case . . ."

"In case what?" I frowned.

"In case whoever went to your house, went to Kelly's next."

I gasped. The doctor paused, asked if I was okay. "Sorry." I waved him on. To Sam, I said. "Why would they—"

He shrugged. "Wouldn't be the first time an officer's family was targeted."

"Oh." I sat back, stunned.

"I'm not saying that it's anything besides an attempted robbery, but sometimes it doesn't hurt to be careful."

"Careful," I murmured.

I wondered if Rob was doing just that.

24

Rob stumbled into the chief's office a little after midnight, bleary-eyed and unshaven. It had been five days since he'd been home.

Five days of sleeping on a disgusting motel floor.

Five days of attending drug riddled parties.

Five days of not getting any closer to solving the case.

Who was bringing the drugs in?

Fuck if he knew at this point.

All he wanted was a bed, a shower, and to sleep for twelve hours.

Chief glanced up from the stack of paperwork. It was their scheduled meet, once a week at midnight, when the station was closed and prying eyes were safely tucked away. "What are you doing here?"

Rob stopped. "It's—"

Chief put up a hand. "I know it's our time. But why aren't you at the hospital?"

Life was funny sometimes. He was literally dragging ass, had barely been able to shake the car tailing him and safely make the drive from Campbell to Darlington. His mind was foggy.

But the moment the word hospital left the Chief's mouth, he was suddenly, abruptly awake.

"What happened?"

"Melissa—"

His gut managed to both unfurl and clench at the same time. Thank God it wasn't the kids, but Melissa. Sweet Melissa with her honey hair, her light brown eyes, her soft smile—

"—house was broken in to. She's hurt."

And that unfurling disappeared completely, his gut twisting itself back into knots, a cold sweat dripping down his spine.

Fuck.

Fuck. Fuck. *Fuck.*

"I gotta go," he said and walked straight out of the office to his car. His personal vehicle was parked at the back of the station lot, hidden in an unused corner with little to no lighting.

It was the perfect place to hide.

Something he'd been doing too damned much of lately, he thought as he got in and cranked the engine.

Music was playing in the background and it was a mindfuck.

Because it was their wedding song.

He was instantly transported back to that day, to promising to love and cherish, to respect and honor—

He'd been doing a fuck-all job of that lately, working on a case, not home, leaving his wife to be injured when he wasn't there to protect her.

Rob tore out of the lot and drove to the hospital.

It only took ten minutes, but they were the longest of his life.

The nurse at the reception desk knew him on sight. If there was one good thing about being a cop, it was that he tended to know the right people in an emergency. "She's in ten."

He nodded and pushed through the door after she'd buzzed him in. His boots clipped against the tile floor as he strode quickly down the hall.

Seven, eight, nine . . . ten.

One inhalation to calm himself before pushing through the

door.

His wife was laughing.

His wife was in another man's arms, laughing. She was pale, but appeared otherwise uninjured.

And she was in another man's arms.

Rob saw red. He stood there like a fucking idiot as a swathe of crimson literally passed over his vision.

Melissa's eyes drifted up from the man—*from the fucking veterinarian*—and finally noticed him standing in the doorway.

"R-Rob?"

"Out," he ordered.

"No."

It wasn't the vet that replied, but another man. This time the one kneeling at Melissa's feet.

He snorted. How fitting.

Then he actually noticed her feet.

And his throat went tight.

They were sliced up like chunks of meat that the doctor was slowly trying to piece back together.

He threaded the needle through the skin, pulling the two sides together.

Melissa winced, bit her lip.

The nurse, a blond in her twenties that Rob didn't recognize, noticed. "Stop," she said. "Feeling's returning."

"Damn." The doctor put down the needle. "I'm sorry we'll have to numb you again. Sometimes it just doesn't work as well in certain patients."

Melissa nodded. "It's okay." She closed her eyes, stiffening and letting out the slightest whimper when the doctor picked up a syringe and pressed it into the sole of her foot.

"Tell me about the time Allie decided to cut open her beanbag," the vet said, clearly trying to distract her, and making Rob feel lower than the dirt on the bottom of his boot.

Melissa's lips twitched. "It was the biggest mess. Looked"— she hissed—"like it had snowed, ah, inside the house."

Rob took a step forward, tired of standing there like a useless idiot.

"I had a dog once that decided to chew mine up," the vet said, gripping her hand and deliberately turning his back on Rob. "Took me three vacuum bags to get it all up." He rubbed her arm. "I still find those little balls in the house sometimes."

Melissa chuckled as she sank back against the bed, the doctor having finished with the syringe. "Me too."

"Why didn't you put her completely under for this?" Rob asked.

The doctor glared. "Because we don't generally need full anesthesia for stitches. Now, keep your comments to yourself, or get out. I want to finish this."

"Maybe you should just step outside until we're done," the nurse said.

"I'm her husband," Rob countered.

The nurse shot him a look that said, "So what?"

He opened his mouth to reply, but Melissa's voice stopped him. "Rob."

A warning. Just like with the kids.

And just like with the kids, it worked.

He dropped into a chair in the corner, sighed heavily, and bit his fucking tongue until it bled.

Then he watched his wife hold the hand of another man.

Watched as she looked to him for comfort.

It was excruciating.

"Shit," Melissa hissed, jerking back.

"Damn," the doctor muttered, reaching for another syringe. "And we were almost done."

"Don't bother with the shot," Melissa said. "That's worse than the stitches."

"You're sure?" the doctor asked.

"Just do it."

"Miss—" Rob began.

She shook her head at him. "Go," she said to the doctor, who nodded and went back to stitching.

Sweat broke out on his wife's forehead, and her normally bright-red lips went ashy gray. The vet didn't try to talk to her then, just held tight to her hand.

The room went silent except for the sound of Melissa's labored breathing, and Rob found himself leaning forward in his seat, gripping his knees in an effort to not jump up and throw the doctor halfway across the hospital for hurting his wife.

He hadn't felt this fucking useless since watching Melissa giving birth to the kids. But at least he'd been the one getting ice chips and holding hands and wiping the tears away.

This was fucking agony.

Then finally it was over.

The doctor stood and pulled off his gloves. "I'll leave discharge instructions with the nurse."

"Haley," the blond nurse said. "Just like I've told you a dozen times."

"Haley," the doctor repeated, either ignoring her sarcasm or exceptionally dense. "Good. Go over the instructions with her."

"Planning on it," Haley muttered as he breezed from the room, white coat flapping behind him and expensive shoes clicking on the tile floor. She began gathering supplies, tossing them, and moving to a computer in the corner.

"He's an asshole."

Melissa's tone sounded almost normal, except for the little waver at the end. And the sheen of tears in her eyes, the paleness of her skin.

"He's very good at what he does." Haley attempted neutrality. Then she rolled her eyes and shrugged. "But he *is* a giant asshole."

Melissa laughed.

It was a real one.

And as that tinkling sound washed over him, warming him from the inside out, Rob realized this is what he'd been missing out on.

25

I squeezed Sam's hand. "You'd better go," I said softly. "Thanks . . . for everything. You didn't have to come." I gave him what I knew was a very watery smile. "To the house for Rocco. Here. You didn't have to stay."

For the first time since I'd met Sam, he looked uncomfortable. "It was nothing."

"It was something to me," I said sincerely and reached up to give him a hug. "Now go back to sleep."

"Unlikely," he said with a short laugh, arms wrapping gently around me. He pulled away. "Rocco's at the hospital, stable and comfortable, but we'll sort out what else he needs in the morning."

"It is morning," I said, glancing up at the clock on the wall.

One side of his mouth curved up. "How about at a more reasonable hour of the morning?"

"Deal," I agreed and waved as Sam left the room, not missing the fact that he and Rob shared a long cold stare before he walked through the door.

Haley wiped her hands on her scrubs. "Well." She sucked a breath through her teeth. "I'm going to get those discharge papers and supplies together."

Traitor.

But she missed my narrow-eyed glare because she was gone.

I glance at Rob, and blurted, "You look terrible."

He rolled his eyes. "Thanks. Good to see you too."

My husband had at least three days of beard growth, and the man could not grow a beard, so his face was covered in uneven patches of prickly-looking hair. Black circles darkened the skin beneath his eyes, which were bloodshot. He'd lost weight and clearly hadn't been eating or drinking properly.

If I didn't know better, I'd think he had a drug problem.

But I did know him. Or, at least I thought I did.

And drugs weren't on the plate of things Rob could tolerate.

"It is good to see you," I said softly. "Hasn't been much of that lately."

He paused, opened his mouth then closed it. His eyes flicked to mine, "What happened?"

That wasn't what he'd been about to say. I'd have bet my last casserole on it. But what was I supposed to do? We were in the middle of a busy hospital, this wasn't exactly the best time to have a discussion about the future of our marriage.

"Someone tried to break into the house."

His face darkened. "Where are the kids?"

"Spending the night as Kel's."

"Do they know what happened?"

"Justin does because Sam called him." His eyes narrowed at my use of Dr. Johnson's first name. "We decided to let Kelly sleep, with the babies and all—"

Rob stood and pushed his hands through his hair. "What babies?"

"I—" My voice faltered. He hadn't been MIA for long, but *God* he'd missed so much. "Kel is pregnant with twins."

"Holy shit," he muttered, pacing the room. "That's—"

"Yeah," I said. "That was my reaction as well. Three kids under four."

"Gross."

I snorted and lay back on the bed, suddenly exhausted. My feet were throbbing more by the second. I wanted painkillers— oral ones this time, because fuck needles—and to sleep for about a decade.

I wanted to wake up and have my life back to normal.

I wanted to wake up and have Rob back.

Talk about gross, I thought, mentally kicking myself in the ass. *Get it together, woman.*

Gentle fingers on my forehead, pushing back locks of hair, stroking the skin behind my ear softly. God, I loved that. "What's wrong?"

"You're not seriously asking me that question, are you?"

Dammit, now tears were leaking out of the corners of my eyes. I'd been strong. I'd held it together, but one flipping touch from Rob, and I was sobbing like a toddler denied an ice cream cone.

I needed his touch, craved his affection, and yet it had nearly destroyed me.

"No," he said. "I wouldn't be stupid enough to do that. Of course not." Dry humor laced his tone, but I wasn't feeling very amused.

When he slipped his arm under my shoulders, preparing to pull me into a hug, I squirmed away. "Not here," I murmured. "I can't. Just not right now."

"But you'll let *Sam* comfort you?" he snapped.

My eyes shot to his, angry and hot. I needed him away from me. I needed him not so close. If he were sweet and kind, if he brushed my tears from my cheeks and held me like he used to, I'd forgive him for everything. I'd forget about these last few months. I'd force the doubts and fury and hurt into the back of my mind, lock the door, and throw away the key. I'd move on and never deal with the issues destroying our relationship from the inside out.

And eventually we'd be right back to where we started.

So I said something to get that distance. Even though it nearly killed me to do so. "Sam's comfort doesn't come with strings."

"You're fucking kidding me, right?" Rob burst out. He turned away, shoulders stiff. "You're fucking kidding me." His hands came up, gripped the back of his head. "How is this my life?"

Haley tentatively walked into the room, discharge papers in hand. "Ready to go home?"

"I don't know," I said softly. "I really don't know."

But I wasn't talking to her. I was talking to Rob.

And he knew it.

26

"*I* need a shower," I said, taking one hobbling step toward the house.

"Wait." Rob closed the door behind me, scooping up the plastic bag with my purse and other belongings inside it. "I'll—"

"I've got it."

Another step. Fuck monkeys, it hurt.

"Let me—"

"*I've got it,*" I snapped. "I'm not weak."

"I never said you were." But Rob didn't argue further, just walked past me and into the house.

I took one more step, nearly crying with the pain, and wondering why in the heck I was insisting on playing the martyr. Not that it mattered, I thought. Rob was gone again. I leaned against the hood of the car, tentatively placed my right foot forward. Red-hot pain sliced through me. "Son of a—"

Maybe crawling would be better.

The door leading into the house was wrenched open, a stool holding the plank of wood back.

Rob marched out, fury in his eyes. His cheeks flushed, his hair a mess. He had the look of a man who'd been pushed too far.

I'd pushed him too far.

My lips parted. A tendril of heat tightened in my stomach. My fingers curled, seeking purchase on the smooth metal of the car.

What the hell, body? This was *not* the time.

He didn't say anything. Not a single word. Not one sound came from his throat.

Instead, he closed the space between us in a matter of heartbeats. His mouth was very close to mine, hot breath puffed on my cheek, my lips. It smelled of the cinnamon gum Rob liked, glazing my tongue, making me yearn for more of the spice against my mouth.

I remembered the first time Rob kissed me. We were all fumbling hands, heat, and teenage desire.

And he had chewed that cinnamon gum.

I'd inhaled the scent, let it soak deep inside me.

Then, just like now, that piece of wholly, intrinsically Rob centered me.

"I . . ."

"Not. One. More. Word." One arm snaked behind my shoulders, the other slipped behind my knees.

He lifted.

One second I was using the car as a crutch, the next I was in his arms, cuddled close to his chest.

Rob had the *best* chest for cuddling, firm and muscular but not too hard. I didn't want to snuggle with granite. I wanted give. I wanted a mix of soft and rigid . . .

Well, at least on his chest I did. Elsewhere I preferred hard all the way.

The absurd thought made me laugh.

I clamped a hand over my mouth when Rob glared down at me.

"What is it?" he gritted out.

"Nothing," I said, but in his arms I felt as though I were floating through a fluffy cloud.

Or maybe being carried on the back of a swan. Flap. Flap. Flap. We went up the stairs.

"I want a shower," I said when he set me on the bed.

"It's already warming up."

"Mmm," I said and grabbed for the hem of my shirt, yanking it up and over my head. Rob had seen it all anyway. My sweats were next. I shoved them down, only slowing when I inched them over my feet so as to not disturb the bandages wrapped around them. My underwear and bra were the last to hit the floor.

I frowned down at my feet. "I'm not supposed to get them wet, am I?"

He cleared his throat, eyes drifting down my body in a way that I might have thought was desire, if he wasn't seemingly interested in a woman like Celeste. A woman who was supposedly all curves and sex appeal and red lipstick and—

"No," he said. "The doctor recommended forty-eight hours. I'll grab a bag. We can wrap your feet in it and top it with a towel. Should be good enough for a quick rinse."

I laid back on the bed, hardly noticing when Rob left. It was hard to concentrate on anything when I was so comfortable. The bed felt like clouds.

More clouds.

I frowned.

I don't think I'd ever compared a surface to clouds and now I'd done it twice in as many minutes.

"Got some," Rob said, coming back into the room with two zip-top bags and a handful of rubber bands.

"Mmm," I said and spread my arms on the duvet. "This is like silk. No." I giggled. "Like clouds."

Rob shook his head. "You'd make a terrible drug addict. They gave you a half tablet of oxycodone and you're high."

"I'm not high," I said, brows pulling down. "This really is as soft as clouds."

"How many times have you thought about clouds in the last five minutes?"

I frowned, and he laughed.

"I guarantee it's been at least five." He circled my ankle and tugged me toward the end of the bed. "You always fixate on one word when you're drunk—though it's not usually clouds, *that* must be a perk of the good drugs."

"I don't fixate on words—"

"Awesome-sauce? Spectacular? Ginormous?" He raised a brow. "Any of those strike up a memory in that pretty mind of yours?"

I crossed my arms. "No."

"Oh, Miss, you're unbelievable." He wrapped the bags and rubber bands around my feet then lifted me from the bed. "You're also the most beautiful thing I have ever seen."

My breath caught. Clouds were pushed from my mind.

"What did you say?" I asked, hesitant. Surely I'd heard wrong. He hadn't—

Rob didn't use words like beautiful. Not to describe me.

"Feet out," he said instead of answering, setting me on the shower floor and adjusting the spray so that warm water splashed down my back. My feet remained outside the door. "Here." Gentle hands tucked a towel around my legs. "I know it isn't the warmest shower, but it's better than nothing, yeah?"

"Yeah," I said softly, knowing in my heart of hearts I wasn't talking about the shower.

"Hair?"

I nodded.

He reached up for the bottles of shampoo and conditioner then helped me wet my hair and wash it. Surreal was the only way to describe this scenario. My head felt full of clouds, and that wasn't the drugs talking. Any side effect of the oxycodone had disappeared at Rob's words.

His hands massaged my hair and shielded my eyes from the suds as he rinsed it clean.

I'd never felt so taken care of. I'd never felt so cherished.

How was that possible when everything was so broken?

He helped me from the shower and to the stool at my vanity. I hated going to bed with my hair wet, and apparently Rob remembered that since he grabbed my blow dryer and comb from the cabinet.

Gentle strokes unknotted the tangles before he stood and gestured to the blow dryer. "I'm helpless with that thing, but I'll grab you some pajamas."

"Rob?" I asked as he moved to the closet.

He turned back. "Do you really think I'm beautiful?"

Silence. Nothing except his eyes on mine, fathomless, his expression incomprehensible.

After a long minute, my eyes dropped to the blow dryer, and I flipped the switch, filling the room with the whooshing noise of air.

But I could have sworn Rob said something, and it sounded an awful lot like, "Yes, Miss. I really do."

27

I didn't do anything fancy with my hair, just blasted the strands until most of the moisture was gone, and when I switched the blow dryer off Rob was back at my side. A long-sleeved shirt and pajama pants in hand.

It was my favorite set, both silky soft and very warm, and very welcome because I was feeling chilled after the whole open-door-shower-situation.

"Ready?" he asked after he'd helped me dress.

I nodded. "Thanks."

Arms around me, a warm chest next to my ear. The bed beneath me, cool sheets, a hot husband . . . who pulled back and tucked the covers around me.

He was leaving.

"Don't," I said before I could stop the word and reached out to grab Rob's arm. I guessed those drugs hadn't completely worn off because normally I wouldn't have asked. I *never* wanted to come across as needy and, dammit, I knew it was important to rely on yourself, first and foremost.

But, the truth was, I didn't want Rob to go.

I wanted my husband next to me. Even if it was all just pretend.

"Please," I murmured.

Someone had broken into the house, Rocco was hurt a second time because of me, my feet were beginning to sting again, and . . . I was so damned lonely.

He pulled away. Slipped from my grip as easily as if it were nothing.

My throat tightened, tears filled my eyes, and I slammed them shut, not wanting them to slip free, not wanting him to see.

It didn't matter.

They slid through my defenses, wet my cheeks, dripping down to soak the cotton of my pillowcase.

Then the bed dipped.

I sucked in a breath. "I—"

"Not tonight," Rob said, wrapping me in his embrace, turning me gently so that my face was pressed against his chest. "Just let me hold you tonight."

My only answer was to scoot closer.

———

I shot to waking a few hours later. Early morning light trickled through the window of my bedroom, and the house was still.

But something had woken me.

I pressed my hand to my chest, trying to calm the racing organ as I sat up and listened.

Then I heard it.

Rob's voice.

It was hushed, barely a masculine rumble.

I glanced at the door, saw it wasn't quite closed. I could just make out the silhouette of one arm raised to his ear. He was on the phone.

My eyes flicked to his nightstand, to his cell on the polished wooden surface.

He was talking on *that* phone.

And we were right back to reality.

"Celeste." Rob's pleading voice raised enough for me to hear it clearly. "Please don't do this."

Pain knifed through me.

And dammit I was tired of this man hurting me. I was on a perpetual merry-go-round of pain and really freaking sick of it.

"Celeste— *Stop*. Listen. You mean too much to me to—"

Fuck. This. Shit.

I threw the covers back and stood.

Then promptly collapsed to the floor in a pile of silk and throbbing limbs. I was an idiot for many things, least of all was forgetting about the fact that my feet were stitched together like Frankenstein's face.

"Moron," I muttered through clenched teeth, flipping over to my hands and knees and crawling my way into the bathroom.

"Please think this through," Rob said just as I reached the end of the carpet and the beginning of the bathroom's freezing cold tile. I'd loved the pale gray shade until I was actually pulling myself across the glossy surface. Nose distance from it, I thought it was really quite ugly.

Or maybe that was my heart talking.

"Don't do anything rash," my husband said to *another* woman just as I closed and locked the bathroom door.

I wriggled my way to my robe and wrestled it on before sitting on the step leading up into our bathtub.

Clean lines, gray and sky blue, double sinks, separate bath and shower, walk-in closet. Cozy white bath mats. A vanity with a gorgeous stool. Fluffy bath sheets . . . and not those tiny towels that hardly covered anything.

The bathroom was a representation of everything I'd ever wanted.

Right?

Rob and I had done nearly all of the work ourselves.

I remembered how proud I'd felt of the space.

We'd done it.

We.

That *we* was gone now.

Plink. A tear dripped down my cheek, dropped to the marble step. Followed by another. And another. And—

"Ugh," I growled, so beyond tired of crying. I was just done. Done with it all.

There was a knock at the door. "Miss?"

I ignored Rob, instead turning on both bath taps to high, letting the sound of the rushing water drown him out.

"Melissa!" I heard him shout.

"I'm fine!" I shouted back.

"Why's the door locked?"

I didn't respond, rotating back to the tub and feeling the water. A bath suddenly sounded like a fabulous idea. I adjusted the temperature, flicked the lever to engage the plug, and began wrestling off my robe and pajamas.

The doorknob rattled. "Let me in."

I snorted. Unlikely.

"Melissa."

"I. Can't. Hear. You," I said lifting myself to the top of the tub before executing some kind of fabulous swing-my-leg-over-with-a-triceps-dip. "Thank you Pilates videos," I murmured.

Thunk.

The door shook in its frame.

"What?" My eyes swiveled toward the pane of wood. Was he really trying—?

Thunk.

Another impact. Another shudder.

"I'm *fine!*" I yelled, not wanting to be down another door.

Rob was either taking his turn to ignore me, or he hadn't heard me because his only answer was another jar against the door. Except this one was followed by a crash as the wood splintered and the lock gave way.

My husband stood, chest heaving, in the doorway. He stepped over the threshold, crunching splinters of wood beneath bare feet as he walked toward me. He wore a pair of old jeans that were as soft as butter, but his eyes were hard and angry.

"What the hell were you doing with the door locked?" he snapped. "You could have hurt yourself, and I wouldn't have been able to help."

I forced my eyes away, studying my toes as I leaned back in the tub. I could almost pretend he wasn't there with the noise of the water drowning out his footsteps.

Unfortunately, it didn't drown out his anger.

That was a pulsing cloud filling the room, weighing down on my chest, my heart.

I was hurting, I was worn down, I was . . . done.

Rob wrenched the taps off, reached across the tub to get right in my face.

"What were you thinking?"

His hair was mussed, twin tracks present from him running his hands through it. His face was slightly flushed, with just the hint of pink on his cheekbones. Hot breath, tinted with cinnamon teased my lips.

It did nothing for me.

It did absolutely . . . everything.

But I couldn't do *this* anymore.

"I want a divorce."

Rob stared at me for a heartbeat.

Just a heartbeat with those scorching black eyes before his mouth was on mine.

28

*R*ob wanted to strangle all of the women in his life.

Least of which his wife.

What was she thinking, walking on her feet? Trying to lift herself into the tub. She could have slipped and cracked her fucking head open, and then where would they be?

"I want a divorce."

His fingers dug fiercely into the granite surrounding the bath, so tightly that he was surprised the stone didn't crack under his grip. What the hell was wrong with her?

A divorce? Really?

He was never going to let that happen.

Rob leaned down, intending to get in her face, to remind her that they weren't this couple, that they made decisions together, that—

Her lips.

God, he'd always loved her lips.

Berry red and plump, they'd always reminded him of raspberries. Or maybe strawberries. She'd been wearing strawberry Chapstick the first time he'd kissed her.

Sweet. Succulent. And way too tempting.

Back then *and* now.

He closed the distance between their mouths. The kiss he gave her wasn't like the ones he typically gave her, not pecks or quick hellos and goodbyes, goodnights, cursory touches to prove that they still loved each other.

This kiss was heat.

It was frustration and anger. It was passion and fury. It was desire and tongue and lips and—

"Fuck!" he shouted, pulling back and bringing one hand up to the corner of his mouth as he sat back on the edge of the tub.

It was teeth.

Melissa's teeth.

Blood was on his fingertips when he pulled them away from his lip. "What the hell, Miss?"

She didn't look at him, instead staring at her toes, which were perched above the water and resting on the edge of granite. Her breathing was hitched and she reached forward to push the lever to drain the tub.

Rob shouldn't stare, but his wife was in front of him naked, and his eyes drifted down her body, noticing every curve, every freckle, every stretch of silky skin. He'd kissed each inch of Melissa a hundred times over.

Just not recently.

Which he suspected was a big part of the problem.

The water drained slowly down her skin, pooling at her breasts then her stomach, then her thighs, then it was gone and she was fully exposed in front of him.

Except for her face.

That was turned away.

He ran a finger down her arm and she jumped, turning farther away from him, her shoulders and hips twisting until she was practically a pretzel in an effort to escape his touch . . . his presence.

"You're—"

"I'm not too skinny, dammit," she screamed, scaring the shit out of him.

He jumped, almost falling from his perch. But then he really looked at his wife, saw what she was doing.

And it nearly broke his heart.

Stiff shoulders. Tense muscles. This wasn't frustration. It wasn't a spat that he could smooth over with a few words.

There was a fucking cavern between them.

How the hell had that happened?

How the hell hadn't he realized it *was* happening?

His voice was quiet. "I was going to say you're beautiful."

Melissa didn't reply, didn't move, didn't look at him.

Rob felt panic crawl into his gut and twist hard. His wife was a live and let live kind of woman. Not much got to her, and even if it did, she was able to compartmentalize it away. To put on a good show and move forward.

She didn't shut down.

Except, a voice niggled, with her mother.

Her mother had hurt Melissa so many times that eventually there hadn't been anything else.

No feelings. No more emotions spent. No energy.

Nothing.

Their relationship had become such an empty shell that when Sonya Harrison had finally left for good, Melissa hadn't cried.

Just as she wasn't crying now.

His gut twisted tighter.

"Melissa," he said and rested his palm on her shoulder.

She stiffened, somehow her delicate little body went even tighter until he could see the striations of her muscles through her skin, until the flesh under his palm felt like the granite around the tub.

He pulled back. Stood.

Would have left if he hadn't seen the relief creep into her frame.

She wasn't as locked down as she would like to portray.

Rob grabbed a towel. One that he remembered fighting with her over in the home goods store. They had been sixty-eight dollars apiece, and he'd abjectly refused to pay that much for a piece of cotton.

Melissa had threatened to never make her chicken and dumplings again.

He'd caved like a cheap suitcase.

They'd bought four of the expensive towels—because she'd needed two, one for her hair and one for her body, and of course they couldn't buy an uneven number of towels—and . . . he loved using them.

They were like silk, cozy and cuddly, and if a man of his profession ever got caught saying, hell just *thinking*, those words, he'd have been razzed out of the department.

He spread the towel over her, hating that she jumped at the contact, then reached into the tub and pulled her into his arms.

She started to squirm, but Rob merely tightened his grip, cognizant of her feet as he maneuvered her from the bathroom, across the carpet, and into their bed.

When he reached for the covers, Melissa tried to scramble from the mattress, but hell if he was going to let her escape now before they hashed this out. There was time, dammit. Even if it meant explaining everything.

"Stop," he muttered, pulling the quilt up and over them both, trapping her legs by throwing one of his over the top.

"Let. Me. Go," she said through gritted teeth as she bucked against him.

Then she cried out in pain and he felt like the biggest jackass on the planet.

"Melissa," he said, pinning her shoulders down and sitting back on her legs to prevent her from getting free. "Stop."

Not that she made it easy on him. She was wilier that Old Man Jacob, and that fucking octogenarian had tried to knee Rob in the balls after getting caught red-handed stealing Betty Jenkins' mailbox.

The entire mailbox.

Rob didn't understand people.

But he understood his wife.

Or he thought he had.

Because he barely recognized the woman beneath him. The coolness in her gaze, the underlying hurt, the stiff body below his.

"Talk, Miss."

She lifted her chin, turned her eyes to the side.

"I'm serious. Either talk or we stay here all day."

He wasn't bluffing.

And she knew it.

29

I stared up at Rob and wanted to smack him.

Of course, to do that I'd actually have to be able to reach him.

Either talk or we're staying here all day.

Ugh. Freaking idiot men.

Did he think he could control me? Did he think he could bend me to his will? Did—

Hell yes, he did.

And why wouldn't he?

I *had* bent. Too many times. Bent and bent and *bent* until I'd felt as though I would break.

No more.

I lifted my chin, made my voice fierce. "If they offer me a contract, I'm taking it."

Rob's brows drew down, forming a little divot I used to love smoothing away. Then again there were a lot of things I used to love doing.

Including my husband.

Who was hot and hard on top of me.

Who knew that restraining me while I was naked would turn me on? Apparently my body was seriously into kink.

Gross.

Except, not gross. Because Rob's stomach was flat, his jeans were unbuttoned and—my eyes flicked down—he wasn't wearing underwear.

I felt like banging my head against the headboard. I probably *would* have if I could have reached it.

He. Is. Screwing. Another. Woman.

I can't be attracted to a man who'd do that to me. I just can't.

But I was.

And Rob knew it.

His eyes darkened. His hips dropped a little heavier against mine, letting me feel the weight of his arousal.

He liked restraining me too.

After all these years, I never would have expected to find something new that pushed both of our buttons.

Rob had always been gentle with me—soft and sweet and tender. I'd liked it, been satisfied . . . when we'd been able to make time to *have* sex with two small kids and a husband who worked insane hours.

But maybe I'd like something more too.

Which was a thought that had never crossed my mind. Not until recently anyway.

I was supposed to be grateful and thankful and whatever else that the universe decreed. My family was safe and healthy. We had food and security and—

Sometimes I wanted more.

Did that make me a bad person?

Maybe. I sighed. *Maybe, it did.*

"I hope you take the contract."

My eyes flew up, collided with Rob's. His were molten, dark and bottomless, inviting me to swim in their depths if only I could find the courage to dive deep into the blackness.

"W-what?"

"If you get an opportunity to do what you love, I want you to take it."

My voice caught in my throat, and then I shook my head.

He lifted one hand from my shoulder, rested it on my cheek. "I'm serious, Melissa."

I pulled away. "I'm serious too. I'm taking it, and it doesn't matter if—"

He bent, slanted his mouth across mine.

This time I didn't bite him. I wanted to. At least for a second. But then his hand slid from my cheek to my chin and held my head in place as he plundered my mouth.

Literally plundered. Like a rake or rogue or pirate.

Or at least that was how I pictured one of those types of men from the historical novels I loved. They took charge in their heroine's bed, making the poor girl—or in this case, my poor *brain cells* fizzle to almost nothing.

Rob's tongue pushed into my mouth, sliding along mine, coaxing, no cajoling, no *demanding* that it tangle with his. He pressed me into the mattress, laying the full weight of his body against mine as his other hand moved from my shoulder to my hip. His fingers were there . . . *almost there.*

I gasped, and he kissed me harder, pressed me firmer, tugged me closer until I didn't know where I ended and he began, until I was kissing him back just as fiercely and wildly.

I yanked at his pants, ripping at the waistband and shoving them down as far as I could reach.

Then he was naked.

"Oh God," I said when he finally released my mouth.

"Yes," he quipped, running his tongue down my stomach, delving it into my belly button.

For once, I didn't feel an ounce self-conscious. This wasn't about stretch marks or saggy boobs or lumps and curves where they shouldn't be. *This* was about heat and feeling and passion and desire.

This was needing my husband's tongue on me, *in* me more than my next breath. This—

"Oh fuuuck." I bucked when Rob pressed his mouth to me

and gripped his hair like it was a steering wheel as I ground against his face.

I don't think I'd ever been this aroused, or at least not this quickly. Of course, it had been months since I'd had a good orgasm.

It wouldn't take months to have this one.

His tongue pressed, his fingers slid home, and I was gone. Flames licked up from my center to explode throughout my body. I glanced down, half expecting to find I'd turned to ash, but ash couldn't feel.

Not the emotions. Not the torment and need and *want*.

Everything with Rob was twisted up, knotted, and so fucking sick.

And I was worse.

Because I wanted him still. I wanted more. I wanted him inside me.

He lifted his head, grabbing the corner of the sheet as he sat up to wipe his face. My eyes slid away from the glistening on his chin, ashamed and turned on at the same time.

"Miss—"

I couldn't.

Not when his voice was that soft. Fuck. Tears burned. My chest rose and fell in rapid movements and not because my husband had just taken me on the fastest, strongest, biggest roller coaster of an orgasm of my life.

I didn't want to feel any of it.

Not the betrayal and agony, not the hope. I wanted to forget it all.

"Sweetheart." A swipe of Rob's thumb along my cheek. "Don't cry—"

I shook off the tendrils of emotion creeping in, the forgiveness for my husband, the urge to forget all and carry on like nothing was wrong.

I would probably hate myself for this, but I didn't want tender. I didn't want my heart involved.

I wanted a rough, raw fuck. I wanted to get lost in sensation and feel nothing but pleasure.

So I brushed his hand from my cheek and reached down between us. He was hot, hard as steel.

His breath hissed between his teeth and he went to pull my fingers away.

I stroked faster, held on tighter.

"Babe—"

"Mmm," I said, need coiling between my legs. I accepted the flames of desire because it cauterized the painful edges of my emotions.

It was all reduced down to rough. To smooth, warm. Wet.

I tugged Rob closer, biting at his neck, scratching his back with my free hand, pulling him tight, accepting him inside.

"Melissa," he groaned.

"Harder," I panted, arching up. Pain bit through my consciousness, my feet not quite ready for the exertion, but my body was. And that slice of hurt put me on the razor's edge. "Rob. Rob. *Rob.*"

"Fuck," he said, pounding into me. "Melissa, please say that you're with me. Please—"

The sheets abraded my back, the pillow bunched under my neck, the blankets tangled at my feet, and I didn't care one bit. Not when the pleasure was twisting, spinning tighter and tighter. "P-lea-se d-don't s-stop." I gasped out, his strokes breaking the words into multiple syllables.

He gripped my hips and stroked harder, deeper than before. His eyes were on mine, burning, excruciating as he took in every detail of my response. I ignored the plea, his need for connection, and focused on his body instead.

The way the cords of his neck strained, his skin shiny with perspiration, the ripple of his abs as he moved in and out, in and out.

And then I didn't have to worry about avoidance.

My eyes slid closed as my orgasm bubbled over and swept through me.

I was barely aware of Rob pounding into me one more time before he cursed and exploded.

I held onto that shield of pleasure as long as possible, gripping tight to the sensation, never wanting to come down.

But I did.

I eventually became aware of Rob on top of me, of my husband stroking my hair and holding me close.

His smell, his body, his touch. Initially, it was only that. Physical. But then my mind cleared, and it all came pouring back in.

Anger. Hurt. Betrayal.

And the worst . . . disgust.

With myself.

30

J shoved at Rob's shoulders, wanting him off me, out of me, away. Far, *far* away.

"Miss—" he began.

I shook my head, squirming harder, shoving more fiercely. "Off," I gasped. "Off now."

"Am I hurting—?"

"Get off me!" I screamed.

Rob's face hardened, but he sat back. I scrambled up, sliding to the side of the bed and swinging my legs to hang off the mattress.

It was only the pull of my stitches that stopped me from standing and running away.

I dropped my head into my hands, hot tears leaking from the corners of my eyes. What had I just done?

A warm palm landed on my shoulder, making me tense up.

"Why are you running?" he asked, as though genuinely perplexed why I might be pulling back from my cheating husband. One whom I'd known was cheating and *still* slept with.

Real freaking smart, Melissa.

"You're kidding right?" I snapped and yanked at the comforter, wrapping it tightly around my body. "Why would I be disgusted for fucking you? *Why?*"

"Disgust—" He snorted in disbelief, shoved to his feet. "That's a really shitty thing to say."

I laughed coldly. "No. A really shitty thing to do was to fuck your coworker and then disappear from our lives. To throw me and our kids away like we didn't fucking matter. *That* was the shitty thing to do."

Rob began pacing, his footsteps pounding even through the thick carpeting. "I've been on a case and couldn't contact you much, but I sent texts for you and the kids every morning and night. You were the one who never responded back."

I wasn't proud of what I did next, but I was a woman at her wit's end.

My fingers wrapped around the heavy protective case surrounding my phone, and I chucked it at my husband's head.

"Then where—" I watched the phone fly and collide with Rob's chest after which it plunked to the carpet. I know, I know, my aim sucked. "Where the fuck are they? Because I never saw a single one."

He bent and scooped the phone up, unlocking the screen before presumably scrolling through my texts.

Then he crossed to his nightstand where there were two phones. He snatched the non-cheater one that we'd picked out at the store together, leaving the other on the polished wood.

He pulled something up on the screen and shoved the phone in my face. "Look."

My eyes flicked down.

I read.

And my stomach twisted into knots.

I still don't know why you're not responding to these, but the case is almost closed. I'll be home soon, and we can talk. I love you and the kids.

I scrolled up, read another text.

I'm sorry about being away so much. I miss you. Tell Max good luck at his game.

I miss you and the kids so much. Being away for work sucks, and I would give anything for some of that blueberry cobbler you were perfecting a few weeks ago.

"It was pie," I murmured before shaking my head at myself. Not the point.

My finger swiped as my eyes rapidly devoured the texts, seeing the words and not understanding. He'd sent them every day, every single day and night. But I'd never received them. Not one.

I love you, Miss. I wish I were home instead of here.

"I don't understand," I said when I'd gotten to the top of the list. "I didn't get any of these."

Rob was scrolling through my phone, reading the texts I'd sent him over the last few weeks. Texts I hadn't received responses to.

"I didn't get any of these either," he said gruffly.

We glanced at each other. What the hell was going on?

Suddenly, he cursed and came around to sit on my side of the bed, snatching the phone from my fingers.

"What—?"

"I just remembered something." He tapped several times on his phone screen, cursed, then tapped a few more times. "Fuck," he said. "Fuck me. She did it. She did it to *me*."

"Who did what?" I asked softly. My heart was starting to pound, hope an unstoppable bubble in my chest. Could it be a misunderstanding? Was it all just technology gone wrong or—

"Celeste fucked with my phone," Rob growled. "She put you on the blocked caller's list and then changed your contact information. Look."

My eyes flicked down, and I frowned at seeing my cell under

the blocked numbers list. It was there, sure as my kids never managed to turn off the lights in their bedrooms. Or bathrooms, or pretty much any room in the house.

But who was to say Rob hadn't put it there?

He sighed at the expression on my face. "I didn't block you, Miss."

"Okay." I nodded even though I didn't feel one hundred percent confident. He'd been so distant these last few months, and this was almost too easy an explanation.

"Want proof?"

I shrugged.

He tapped at the screen again, pulling up the contacts section and scrolling down. When he stopped at W my heart caught.

Because there were two listings for wife.

One was "Wife." The other was "wife."

"Capital Wife" was the blocked listing. Rob flicked backed to the messages screen and sure enough "lowercase wife" was the number he was texting. It should have been my number, but when he clicked on the little circle near the top of the message chain, I saw that it didn't match my cell phone.

"I know this number," he said pointing at the screen, "because it's Celeste's work cell."

"And you just know Celeste's work number?"

Rob raised a brow. "We've worked closely together these last few months."

I snorted. "Yeah. I know."

"What's that supposed to mean?"

"Only that it's obvious to everyone in this town that you've mixed duty with a slice of on-the-job-pleasure and that Celeste was your favorite version of it."

"That's bullshit."

I stopped and glared at him. "Oh, so you haven't kissed her? Had your hands on her and her hands on you? You haven't touched or fantasized or *fucked* her?"

"What?" Rob jumped to his feet. "Of course I haven't."

"Rob." I sighed and stared up at him. "Aside from the lipstick on your collar that you came home to *me* with, you were seen."

His shoulders hunched up, protective and defensive at once, and that churning disgust made a comeback, twisting my gut, raising my blood pressure.

"I haven't slept with her," he muttered. "And any touching or kissing was strictly for the case."

"That according to you? How does she feel about it?" He froze and so did my heart. "Yeah," I murmured. "That's what I thought."

"Celeste can be a little persistent, but she knew I was married. That everything had to be on the level. We only pretended to be a couple when it was necessary to further the case."

The case. The God damned case.

My fingers clenched on the comforter. "Was the case so important that it was worth ruining us?"

Rob sank onto the bed next to me and took my hand. "It didn't ruin us. We're in a rough patch is all."

"My husband has been accusing me of cheating on him with our vet, when he's been pretending to sleep around with his beautiful coworker. Further, he—*you*—" I glared fiercely at him. "You deprioritized me and our kids until we had to either stop missing you or learn to live without you. And none of that goes into the lack of clarity you have about what the kids and I have been going through or addresses the jealousy or justifies the fact that you tried to stifle my dream." I flopped back and stared up at the ceiling. "What am I supposed to say, Rob? Oh, there was a cell phone snafu, everything's fine now?"

"I—"

"Because none of it is fine." I plunked my hands over my face. "It all sucks. I'm lonely and hurt and disgusted that I still want you. The kids miss you. They miss their dad who used to come to sporting events and school plays. I miss the man who didn't freeze me out and shut me down at every turn."

"I had to," Rob said. "I couldn't risk bringing our family into the case."

I propped my elbows beneath me. "Why not?"

His face closed down, and I knew that I would never get the answer that I might hope for, never get the explanation or understand if it was all truly worth it.

"Never mind," I said. "I get it. I'll never be worthy enough to confide in. I understand that I'm not part of"—I made air quotes —"the sheriff club and couldn't possibly understand all the idiosyncrasies of police work, but I was here, waiting and willing to be by your side." My voice broke. "If only you hadn't thrown me away."

"I didn't—"

"I don't understand why you're still here." I spread my legs and pointed between them. "Are you that desperate for another lay? Have another itch for me to scratch since Celeste isn't here?"

"Miss. I haven't—"

"Fuck off, Rob. Just fuck the hell off."

I interrupted him because it was easier to do that than allow his slick, charm-filled lies to fill my heart. It was easier to pull back and have distance rather than face the truth.

My family was imploding.

31

*H*e needed to come clean.

About everything.

If Rob wanted to keep his wife, he needed to tell her everything.

The investigation, the drugs, the kisses, and touches. He had to lay it all on the table and not leave out a single detail.

Because if she found out later that he'd glossed something over, any trust he'd earned back would be gone.

"Miss," he said, talking louder and faster when she would have probably interrupted to tell him to fuck off again—and rightly so, he had to admit. "Three months ago there were a series of robberies in Darlington, do you remember?"

She paused and he held his breath.

"Yes," she replied after a long moment.

"They were connected to a crime ring that was interwoven throughout the entire Tri-Hills area." Her brows pulled down and he added, "Darlington is still relatively safe. The burglaries were on the outskirts of town, if you recall?" She nodded. "But things are getting bad in Campbell and Douglasville and that's spilling over here at home."

"Has anyone been hurt?"

His heart squeezed. God he loved his wife. "Yes. A nineteen-year-old girl was murdered. She was blond with light brown eyes and a sweet face."

Her exhale was shaky, and he took a chance.

Careful to keep the blanket wrapped around her, he slid over and pressed his shoulder against hers. "Yes, she reminded me of you. Before Max and Allie. Before this house. A blameless girl who'd been hurt, and I vowed that no more innocents would be caught in the crossfire. But that's not everything, because she also reminded me of Allie and Callie and loads of others. I just couldn't get that girl out of my head." He placed his hand over Melissa's. "So when Celeste came to me with a plan that bordered on risky, I took it to the chief."

"Why was it risky?"

"No badge, no weapon, no backup. Chief was convinced that someone on the inside was easing the dealer's way. So it was just Celeste and me to watch each other's backs as we tried to infiltrate the gang. Problem was what we initially thought was just a couple of backwoods meth labs turned out to be a huge ring of cocaine dealers." Her hand twitched. "Yes," he said softly. "Big money, big crime, and big time over our heads. Which is why I was coming in tonight to tell the chief that we needed to pull out and involve the FBI. But—"

"Celeste wasn't happy."

Rob risked linking his fingers with hers. Melissa didn't pull away. "No, she wasn't. But the break-in here couldn't have been a coincidence." He swallowed hard, his voice gruff. "Now I'm worried I might have brought something huge down onto our heads."

"The kids—"

"They're safe at the ranch," he assured her. "I spoke to Justin before Celeste, and he's aware of what's happening. Between the extra patrols from the department and the private security he called in, that place is locked down tighter than Fort Knox."

"But—"

"They're fine, and you will be too once I get you there."

She nodded but didn't say anything for a long time. And when she did eventually speak it wasn't what he expected.

"Can you grab me some clothes?"

"I—"

Pale brown eyes flashed up to his, slender fingers scrunched the floral pattern on their bedspread. "I'm aware there is more we need to talk about," she said, her tone bordering on ice. "But this isn't exactly a conversation I want to have while I'm naked."

"I like you naked," he said.

Her eyes warmed for a second before her face closed down. "Yeah."

Rob bent to catch her gaze with his own. "Miss?"

She shook her head. "Now isn't the time for that conversation. There are more important things we need to talk about."

"Maybe." He caught her chin when she tried to look away. "But why did that hurt you?"

Tears made her eyes glassy. "It doesn't matter." A shrug. "It's an old hurt anyway."

"This conversation is going to take all night if I keep having to tear the information out of you."

That startled her into a laugh. "I guess so, huh?" She sighed. "It's just that I don't think you've said that you liked my body the way it is in a long, long time. I'm always too thin or I need to eat more, or you won't let me forget the one time I let anxiety get the best of me, and I stopped eating."

"What?" He sat back on the bed, genuinely surprised. "I love your body. I say you're beautiful all the time."

Melissa bit her lip. "I don't want to be a jerk here, but think for a second and tell me honestly if you can remember a time when either of us talked about anything other than the kids or their school or getting them to some extracurricular activity." She gripped the blanket tighter, and Rob got up to grab her a tank top and a pair of pajama pants. He'd been hurting his wife for a very long while. The least he could do was get her some clothes.

"And I'm not innocent either," she said, her words coming fast as he walked back to the bed, clothes in hand. She always did that when she struck a blow in an argument. Tried to make everything else a little softer, tried to shoulder extra blame so that he would somehow feel less culpable.

But her words were the truth.

When was the last time he'd looked at Melissa as his wife first and not the mother of his kids?

Those two facts were inexorably tied together, and so that made them impossible to separate. Except . . . when was the last time that he'd just thought of her as the woman he loved?

Years.

"We've been drifting apart, and I haven't been good at bringing us together," she said. "I let the blog and TV show come between us."

He helped Melissa slip the tank top over her head then carefully guided her pajamas up and over her feet.

"I'm not jealous of the blog." He guided the pants past her hips. "And I meant it when I said that I want you to do the show. I do. I was worried about the exposure, that someone might connect something, and it would put you and the kids at risk." He laughed bitterly. "Turned out that I was able to do that all on my own, no media presence necessary."

He tucked the comforter around her, the weight of all the ways he'd hurt her bearing down on him.

Damn, he'd really fucked this whole thing up.

"Miss?"

She cocked her head to the side, probably because the nickname was so rasped out that it was barely recognizable.

"Yeah?"

"Maybe you should divorce me."

Good God, he couldn't even get that out correctly. Couldn't even man up and say what he was thinking. She should dump his ass and move on with her life, find someone to take care of her— almost any jackass would do a better job of it. Melissa needed to find someone to appreciate the gorgeous, loving, selfless, amazing woman she was.

That someone hadn't been him, and yet he hoped, *hoped* that she might forgive him.

So her next words gutted him.

"I probably should."

y feet ached, my stitches burned, and my heart felt as though it had been shattered then pieced agonizingly back together.

Bruised. Tender. And somehow whole again.

"Rob," I said when he nodded and stood, obviously not understanding my previous words, not hearing the "should" as I had.

I should, but I couldn't. Not when the whole situation was twisted but unintended, agony without malice.

He froze at the sound of his name on my lips, looking back at me with dark eyes devoid of hope.

And that hurt perhaps more than anything else.

Rob was my husband, but he was also a man who couldn't abide failure—his, not others.

Other people's failures he understood.

His? Those were unforgivable.

I knew he'd be much, much slower to forgive himself than I would.

Maybe it was my childhood. Maybe it was the fact that I'd been hurt over and over and *over* again by my mother. Maybe I was just beyond screwed up and incurably distant.

But . . . I could compartmentalize the hurt away. Tuck it deep down until it wasn't festering and instead was only a throb and then a pulse. Shove it away until it was nothing and then continue on living my life.

God, I was so screwed up.

"No, you're not," Rob said, and I blinked, realizing that I'd spoken aloud.

"Yes, I am." I put my hands on the bed, ready to push up to standing only to remember . . . my feet. *Argh.*

"This is so annoying!" I smacked my palms against the mattress, the sharp noise extremely satisfying when nothing else in my life seemed to be. Okay, well not *nothing* else. Fifteen minutes ago had been pretty freaking satisfying. It's just that I wanted to stand up. I wanted to *move.*

Toward Rob.

But I didn't know exactly how to do that. Could we really put the last couple of months behind us?

Logically, I understood.

Internally, my heart still throbbed.

I couldn't quite justify or comprehend how exactly we'd allowed ourselves to be pushed apart. What if the whole sick pattern repeated itself during his next case?

"What's annoying, baby?" he asked.

"I want—"

"Shh." His hand came up, covering my mouth. Which was pretty damn rude, thank you very much. I started to pull it off when I noticed his body. His jaw was clenched, his shoulders up and taut, and every muscle from his brows down to his toes was locked and loaded, ready to spring.

"Fuck," he hissed, eyes on the door, on me, on the bedroom. "I'm going to take my hand off, quiet okay?"

I nodded.

The hand was gone in an instant, and he was at the door in the next, closing it, engaging the lock with a click, and flicking off the light.

I wanted to ask what the hell was happening, but Rob was in cop mode and I'd promised him quiet.

And I'd never seen him like this, aggressive, catlike, silent but carefully coiled and ready to strike.

"Closet," he mouthed, scooping me up around the waist and carrying me through the bathroom.

I cursed my feet again even as I felt one hundred percent secure in his arms.

It's just that I wanted to be helpful. I didn't want to be one of those idiot fictional women who turned to the male lead and said, "What do we do now?"

Even though I was barely stifling the urge to do so.

At least until I heard the noises. Glass breaking. Footsteps pounding.

"Text dispatch," Rob said, setting me down in the closet and closing that door. Which didn't have a lock.

He slid our dresser in front of it, pressed four quick buttons on the safe on the wall—the one that held his service weapon, which I'd insisted on because of the kids—and pulled out his gun.

The *click* of the safety being removed sent a shiver down my spine.

"Miss."

I looked up into black eyes. The closet was dark, his face barely visible, but I could picture his eyes in my brain. They'd be kind but intense. Telling me to move my ass . . . but in a nice way, if that was even possible.

"Text them. Now." He listed a series of numbers and our address, which I dutifully typed into the phone and hit send. "Good," he said, and hunkered down in front of me, carefully sliding us into the deepest corner of the closet. Back behind our winter parkas and ski pants, behind our summer clothes—many months from rotation again—back until my spine hit the wall.

The smell was slightly musty, and as patently ridiculous as it was, I actually made a mental note to pick up an air freshener for the space.

Bad guys were invading our house, and I was making a shopping list.

That was some kind of screwed up.

But before my mental list got longer, I heard it.

Or rather *them*. On the stairs.

Rob seemed to get impossibly tenser, his body shielding mine as we heard the footsteps pound closer. They weren't bothering to be quiet. Instead they clumped through the hall, slamming doors, breaking things.

I mentally followed the footfalls through the second floor. Into Max's room. Then Allie's. And once again, I was beyond grateful for my sister.

Thank God my kids were not here.

Eventually the sound made it to our room.

I heard male voices and felt the house vibrate as they crashed against the door.

"That'll make three ruined doors in one day," I muttered.

Rob huffed out a laugh, shifting slightly in front of me as the crash reverberated through the walls.

"Stay behind me," he whispered. "No matter what."

My heart clenched. I nodded.

"Promise."

"Promise," I whispered.

And then the closet door shuddered.

$\mathcal{I}$ watched the silver handles of the dresser rattle as the door was inched irrevocably forward. They rose and fell to the wood surface making a tinkle that was way too delicate for the current situation.

Then I heard them.

Quite possibly the best sound on the planet.

Sirens.

Quietly at first then louder.

The gap was wide enough now for the barrel of a gun to peak through into the closet. That black metal tube might have been the most frightening thing I'd ever experienced.

I worried it would gain enough purchase to turn and point at Rob. Then aim and pull the trigger and—

A curse rent the space, and the gun suddenly disappeared.

Footsteps pounded away from the closet, down the stairs, out across the back deck.

Blowing out a relieved breath, I started to rise to my knees.

Rob shook his head, placed a hand on my shoulder to steady me.

That was when I heard them.

Softer footfalls out of the bathroom, hitting the creaking step on the flight of stairs, slipping out the back door.

A chill slid down my spine, and my teeth chattered.

There was something immensely terrifying about the casual pace of the last intruder, as though they didn't care about the police sirens bearing down on the house, that froze my blood.

I didn't like it.

Didn't like the feeling it gave me.

But I didn't have a lot of time to process that emotion because there was a whole other series of crashing and banging and pounding footsteps.

"Police!" The dresser rattled again.

"Identify yourself!" Rob shouted.

"Rob?"

Rob sighed and stood. "Hayden," he said to me. "Yup," he called. "I'm going to move the dresser so we can come out."

Sticking his gun into the waistband of his jeans, he shifted the set of drawers back and out of the way. Then he flicked on the light, waited a moment, seemingly to allow his eyes to adjust to the sudden brightness, and cracked the door.

I was still blinking against the spots of white in my vision when Hayden stuck his head into the closet.

"Everyone okay?" His gun was still drawn, but resting at his side.

"We're fine," Rob said. "I need to get Melissa out to the ranch and talk to Celeste."

Hayden's eyes cooled, flicked to me crawling my way out of the corner. "I think that—"

I ignored them both, trying to pretend the flicker of pain at the mention of her name didn't actually hurt. I had clarity now, and while everything in our marriage wasn't magically fixed or perfect or hell, even average at this point, I understood the situation better.

I was just storing all the information aside until later when I could decompress and process. When I wasn't bra-less in a house filled with police officers who'd just managed to unwittingly scare away some men who wanted to seriously hurt us.

Or that was what I presumed, anyhow.

For now, I wanted to get the hell out of this house, get to Kelly's and hug my kids tight.

I wanted to pretend that there wasn't a drug ring the next town over. That my husband hadn't disappeared on me, only to reappear and try to play shining knight.

I wanted to concentrate on the fact that I might have a shot at my dream and that Max might score a goal in his next soccer game, and that I was totally going to let Allie enter that equestrian tournament she'd been begging me about.

I was going to pretend my house wasn't full of three broken doors, who knew how much shattered glass and ransacked drawers.

I was going to go and hug my kids.

Reaching up, I snagged my rattiest, coziest sweatshirt, yanked it from its hanger, and slipped it over my head.

"Let's go," I said, hobbling over to Rob.

"Miss." He frowned, glancing down at my feet. "You shouldn't—"

"We're going," I gritted out. "Now."

I was a woman on the edge. I'd been pushed too far.

Terrorized in my own home. Twice. A husband who withheld information to *protect me*.

Yes, there were mental air quotes on that.

"Melissa—"

"Now, Rob, God dammit!"

I smiled sweetly at Hayden, even as I shoved past him rudely. I'd probably be embarrassed by my actions later.

But I'd. Had. Enough.

"Bye, Hayden."

"Bye, Miss."

Ouch. Ouch. Each step was ridiculously painful. I was probably due a pain pill, but I didn't want to take the time. So I moved on my heels like some sort of deranged mummy and used every handhold and surface I could reach to help disperse my weight.

And I made it as far as the bathroom sink before I found myself slung up and over Rob's shoulder.

I grunted as all the air whooshed out of my lungs. "What are you doing—?"

"I miss my sweet wife," he muttered, navigating us to the bedroom and then down the stairs. "Where did she go?"

"You—" I fought his grip, nearly sending us both down the remaining steps.

Rob cursed, clamped me tighter against him, and finished the descent. "She used to be so easygoing, so caring. Now all I get is a fight." Louder, he said, "McMann, I'm taking her to Kelly's then I'll come back to give a statement."

"Roger that," McMann responded, and I could hear the amusement in his tone.

Asshole.

Out the front door, down the porch steps, and Rob continued talking. "A nice wife. A family. All I ever wanted. All I ever needed. Instead I get this—"

He popped me on the ass.

The *crack* didn't hurt, but it did make me see red.

And it made me do something I never thought I'd do.

I socked him.

Hard and right in the kidney.

"Oof."

All of a sudden I was right side up, having made a not so gentle landing in the passenger seat of my minivan.

Rob rubbed his back, and though I felt guilty, I couldn't bring myself to apologize.

After a moment, he crouched in front of me. His hands were on my knees, his eyes level with mine. "All I ever wanted was you, Miss."

I turned my head away.

"I like it when you punch me."

Shocked, my gaze whipped back to his.

"What—"

"I like it when you get angry." His palm came up to cup my cheek. "I like it when you're pissed off. I love it when you lecture me on the finer arts of baking powder versus baking soda."

I sniffed, opened my mouth to retort—

His lips brushed mine, softly, gently, a barely-there caress that was gone almost before my brain processed it had happened.

"I like it when you're angry because it means you care."

34

I brushed back Max's hair and pressed a kiss to his forehead. He was hot, that special kind of inferno that kids always seemed to radiate when they're sleeping.

He sighed, rolled to his side, wriggling deeper underneath the covers.

"Love you, snuggle bug."

Had he been awake, I would have received an eye roll in return, but since he was dead to the world and I'd just been through a potentially life-threatening situation, I figured I had Mom Cred.

In that, I was allowed to use whatever cheesy nicknames for my kids I wanted.

"Mom?"

I jumped when Max's eyes flew open and he stared up at me.

"Yeah, bud," I murmured. "I just got here so I thought I'd come in and say good night."

"M'kay." His lids drooped.

"Love you." I pressed another kiss, shoved up to my heels and shuffled through the Jack and Jill bathroom to Allie's room.

I wondered briefly if they'd have to give the bedrooms up when the twins were born, before internally chuckling. There were at least another six unused bedrooms at the ranch. Kel and Justin would have to make a lot more babies before my kiddos had to give up the privilege of their own room at Auntie Kel's house.

Also, this just in: thinking of my sister procreating was gross.

I rolled my eyes, gripped the doorframe, and made my way over to Allie's bed. I found that walking on my heels wasn't so bad.

She was sleeping on her back, arms and legs spread eagle, little body taking up as much of the mattress space as physically possible. She'd kicked the blankets off, so I pulled them up and tucked them tightly around her.

No doubt they'd be in a pile at the foot of the bed in no time, but I couldn't just let her stay uncovered.

She might get cold.

I leaned close, brushed a finger down one soft cheek, and pushed a strand of hair off her forehead. Her breaths were long and even, laced with the scent of her bubblegum mouthwash.

"Night, sweet pea," I whispered and tucked Mr. Tails, her ratty stuffed cat, under the blankets with her before stepping back.

Allie didn't reply, her sleep unhindered by my fussing. I limped my way out of the room and closed the door behind me.

Then nearly screamed when I saw the man in the hallway.

"Sorry, I didn't mean to startle you," he said softly. "I'm Danny with the security company. I wanted to introduce myself. I'll be on patrol inside all night."

My heart was thundering, and I placed my hand on my chest to steady it. "I'm Melissa," I said, happy my voice sounded relatively even. I mean the man was a giant. Several inches taller than Rob, and with arms that resembled tree trunks. Add in the tattoos and—I forced my eyes away—was that a bullet wound on his neck?

Or a freshly healed over one, anyway.

Holy soufflé. Just what kind of people did Justin know?

"Nice to meet you," I said into the silence that had fallen.

What did one say to a man who looked like he could crunch you into a million pieces? He was going to petrify the kids.

But then Danny smiled, and I saw a kindness in his eyes that instantly put me at ease.

Okay, maybe he wouldn't frighten the kids so long as he kept that grin at the ready.

Danny extended an arm and handed me a cell phone.

It wasn't mine.

"Uhh," I said eloquently, even as I took the phone. It was the latest model of i-whatever and way nicer than my cracked screen, super old and slow version.

"A clean line." He shrugged. "Just in case. Your contacts are preprogrammed. And if you need anything, security is speed dial under one."

"Okay." I stared at the blank home screen, half-expecting to see my picture of the kids and Rob and somehow disappointed when I didn't.

"Or you can text."

I nodded. Of course they wouldn't load family pictures on the phone.

But why then did it feel so wrong that they weren't there?

Ignoring the niggling, I thanked Danny and slipped past him.

Since I wasn't usually invited for sleepovers at my sister's house, I didn't have my own room. But Justin had said I could sleep in the empty bedroom directly across the hall from the kids. And no surprise, it was gorgeous, filled with expensive furniture I could never dream of owning and linens that probably cost more than my car.

Not that expensive furnishings and sheets were Justin's thing any more than they were Kel's, but Justin's family was old money, and that meant they came with things like a live-in housekeeper and thousand-thread count towels.

My sister had definitely moved up several spheres in the social echelon since Justin had come around.

But silky sheets and a luxurious mattress weren't necessary

tonight. I was beyond exhausted from the events of the last day, and I would surely have fallen asleep no matter where my head landed.

After hobbling to the bedside, I pulled back the comforter and swayed a little. Given the swirling sensation in my head, the pain pill that Justin had forced on me must be starting to work.

But only just, I supposed, since I didn't have the urge yet to talk about clouds.

I wrinkled my nose, flipped off the bedside light, and flopped onto the pillows, tugging the blankets up and carefully slipping my feet beneath them.

Not even one day as an invalid, and I was already sick of it.

How was I supposed to parent if I could barely walk?

And it wasn't even like I had a broken limb and could manage on the other leg. Nope, I'd managed to mangle the bottoms of both feet.

Brilliant. Excellent work, Miss.

Sighing, I closed my eyes and waited for sleep to overtake me.

Son of a beignet, mother fillet of tilapia, and whatever other culinary curse words I could come up with—I really needed to curb my current penchant for the f-bomb if I didn't want to risk the kids picking it up. That thought was mute at the moment though, because my brain had decided that despite two break-ins in less than twelve hours, one ER visit complete with stitches, glue, and irrigation, and then some seriously way too adult and contentious conversations with my husband, it was not going to let me sleep.

No. It wanted to pour over every detail of the intrusions, of the words exchanged with Rob.

It wanted to focus on the sex. Which had been—

I bit my lip.

Really, really good.

My mind deconstructing each detail of the night was probably the only reason I heard Rob slip into my room.

I knew instantly it was him, in the way that a person's body knows another body as well as their own. Sudden awareness, a flash of heat, of comfort, and still, unfortunately, a small slice of hurt.

He was almost silent because Justin's house didn't have squeaky floors or unoiled hinges, but despite the darkness, I could track his movements. The careful closing of the door, the soft footsteps across the carpet, the careful descent . . . into the chair near the foot of the bed.

"No," I said and felt him freeze. "Here." I lifted one side of the comforter.

After a second, I heard him push to his feet. Then he was fully clothed in bed next to me.

But it was okay because he pulled me into his arms, held me tight to his chest.

It was okay because he was Rob, because he was my husband, because he smelled good, and his chest was the same soft-hard combination of man that had given me comfort so many times over.

"You were wrong to do what you did," I said.

His lungs expanded and compressed beneath my ear. "Yes, I was."

And then I fell headlong into sleep.

35

"*B*ut Mom!"

I crossed my arms and glared down at my daughter. "Absolutely not."

It was Saturday evening, one day after the events from hell, and I'd just woken up. Which was totally going to mess my brain up for the week, but sleep schedules aside, my mom duties didn't end.

"Your Aunt Kelly isn't feeling well," I reminded her. We'd taken that route rather than explain it was because of a security risk that we couldn't allow Allie to go for a ride.

"Uncle Justin can—"

"Your Uncle is taking care of Abby and—"

"Allie."

Rob's voice warmed a trail down my spine. I glanced over my shoulder. He'd been gone when I'd woken up, but had reappeared like magic to carry me downstairs and settle me on the couch.

When I'd protested my feet were feeling better after the full day's rest, he'd simply rolled his eyes and lifted me up into his arms.

Then he'd tucked a pillow behind my back, settled a blanket

over my middle, and handed me my dose of antibiotic along with a glass of water.

"Your mother said no." Rob crossed his arms. "So it's no."

I saw the explosion brewing before Rob did.

Cheeks going red, lips pressing tightly together before her chest filled with air.

"It's *not* fair."

"Sweetheart," I said. "We've talked about this. Sometimes things don't go to plan, and we have to make changes on the fly."

I purposely used an idiom I didn't think she'd understand, hoping the confusion and her typically incessant need for questions would diminish some of her anger.

Maybe it wouldn't always work, but it did this time.

"Why are you talking about a fly?" Her skin was still flushed but not nearly as much as before, and instead of tears in her eyes, she had questions.

"*On* the fly, honey," I said, grabbing her hand and pulling her close so I could cuddle her against my chest. Sometimes there was nothing better than the smell and feel of your kid. Soft and fragile and so, *so* precious.

Last night had reminded me of that. For a moment, I thought I'd never get to see her again, never get to hold her.

Even if she was going right back to driving me crazy less than twenty-four hours later.

"It means that sometimes things change without reason, and we can't control them. It means that we can't get upset about it." I held her pale brown eyes with my own. "We can be disappointed, but it also means we can't throw a temper tantrum because we understand that stuff sometimes happens."

Her brows pulled together, and I waited as she processed my words.

"You mean like when I spilled the milk?"

My lips twitched. "Which time?"

She giggled. "When you were going to make Max's birthday cake."

I nodded. "Yup. Just like that. Did it bother me at all?"

Her head bobbed like a marionette. "Oh yeah."

"But did I get mad about it? Did I yell at you?"

"No." She frowned. "You helped me clean it up, and . . ." I watched her mind work, smiling at the little v that formed between her eyebrows as she concentrated. "We went and bought more milk."

"Exactly." I stroked her hair back. "There was an issue, and we made the best of it. Max got his birthday cake a little late, and you helped me make the decorations a little extra special, right?"

"Right." Allie nodded firmly. "So Aunt Kelly and Uncle Justin can't go with me. But I can go by myself!"

She started to push off me.

I snagged her arm and sighed.

Sometimes when you thought you had it all figured out as a parent, your kid decided to throw you a curveball.

———

"AND SHE COULDN'T DECIDE if she wanted to be a land narwhal or a sea unicorn . . ." I read to Allie a few hours later.

"Look!" She pointed at the picture. "Rainbows come out of her horn."

"That's cool," I said and read on about the little unicorn that couldn't decide where she belonged, but discovered in the end that sometimes the place you end up belonging might be the place you least expect.

Damn. Sometimes kids' books were deep.

My lips twitched, and I glanced over at Rob who was sitting on the floor next to the bed and reading emails on his cell phone.

Not *that* cell phone, thankfully. Though my stomach still clenched at the thought of Celeste and the case and what Rob had actually done with her in the name of "case work."

He must have felt my gaze on him, because he put the phone down and met my eyes. His were earnest, the typically unfathomable black depths, strangely clear, and I knew it was his attempt at a truce, at putting the past behind us.

See, they seemed to be saying. I'm not a mystery. I have nothing to hide.

I wanted to believe that. For sure, I did. It would be simpler for me to shove it all away and just move forward, but I couldn't help but feel as though something between us was irrevocably changed.

And based on the way his eyes flitted from mine, focusing on the plush area rug near Allie's bed, he seemed to think the same.

Sighing, I closed the book and fussed with Allie's blankets, tucking her and the ragged Mr. Tails under her arm and pressing a kiss to her forehead.

"Night, sweetie," I said and carefully found my feet.

Rob stood, no doubt to continue carrying me around the house like I was his personal parcel, but I waved him away. Justin had brought me the crutches we'd forgotten at the hospital, and I could maneuver fairly easily between them and walking on my heels.

Much easier than the previous night, that was for sure.

I bent, snagged them up, and slid them under my arms. "I'm going to say goodnight to Max."

Carefully, I maneuvered through the shared bathroom and into Max's bedroom. He was lying on his floor, reading a graphic novel about underwear and a superhero. I rolled my eyes, wondered how many times he'd reread that one, and said, "Time for bed, little dude."

"Aw, Mom!" he groaned.

"Nope," I said, crutching closer. "No whining. It's late and it's lights out."

He wrinkled his nose, but set the book aside and crawled into bed.

I put the crutches on the floor and perched next to him. This was usually our time for a chat about the day or whatever random topic he decided he wanted to quiz me on. I'd already discussed the three branches of government, global warming, and the qualities of diamonds versus gold—and that was just this week.

Thank God for our local library, or I would have never survived the inquiries. Me not knowing the answer to his plethora of questions made for a great excuse to visit.

But today he didn't ask me about executive privilege or when the national parks were first established. Today, he asked me something much harder.

"Are you and Dad going to be okay?"

My throat tightened. Especially when he stared up at me, his eyes so similar to Rob's.

He was a mini-me of my husband, a portal to the past, to how Rob and I had been twenty years earlier.

And it was that history that made the question both the easiest and the hardest of my life to answer.

I tucked the blankets up to his chin, reached to pull the bottom up, exposing his feet to the fresh air.

Another thing that was just like his dad.

I smiled down at Max, knew in my heart my words were the truth. "Yes, buddy. We'll be okay."

36

I'd just wobbled my way into the kitchen when Kelly walked in through the back door. She was trailed by two men from the security company Justin had hired.

"Hey," she said as I plunked myself into one of her wooden chairs and set my crutches within arm's reach. "You're awake."

"I am."

She grabbed a bowl of watermelon from the fridge and came over to sit at the table with me. Her eyes flicked to Rob, who was standing guard behind my right shoulder and didn't seem to plan on sitting any time soon.

"How are your feet?"

A shrug. "Better than expected. Can you tell Justin thanks for the crutches?"

She nodded, squeezed my hand, and dug into the melon.

I smiled. "Can I risk snagging a piece? Or will you gnaw off my fingers?"

"Funny," she said, a dribble of juice running down her chin. "These babies, they just make me so hungry all the time." She paused, her hand coming to her stomach. "Either that or nauseous. *Ugh.*" She pushed the bowl away, wiped her mouth, and leaned her head back to glance at the ceiling.

"Rob," I said and all but shoved the bowl at him. "Take that away and grab the saltines from the pantry. They're on the top shelf."

"I haven't had time to go to the store," she said.

I carefully patted Kel's knee. "I hid an extra box in there last time I was over." I smiled when her relieved eyes met mine. "For emergencies just like this."

Rob was back before I finished speaking, a sleeve of the cardboard-like crackers in hand.

I swear, there was nothing better for any stomach ailment than saltines.

I opened the package, thrust a few crackers at Kel, and turned to ask Rob for a glass of water, but he was already there, cup in hand.

Without a word, he set it within Kel's reach.

My eyes shot to his, and I felt the band around my heart, my lungs—the one that had been making it impossible for me to breathe, to feel anything deeply . . . I finally felt that band snap.

I had to look down, to take a couple of deep inhalations as I studied the grain pattern on the table and willed the tears away.

Was it relief I felt? Or fear?

Fear that I'd opened myself up to Rob again, that I couldn't continue to hold myself separate and safe.

That I'd go back to being the Melissa of the last few months.

Shut down. Distant. Weak.

Rob cupped my jaw in his palm. He shook his head, just once, as though he knew what I was thinking . . . as though to say, "Never again."

And then he kissed me.

It could have been our first kiss all over again. His lips were so gentle, so softly coaxing against mine. As if he were scared I'd pull away. As if he had to convince me to stay and give him a chance.

But here was the thing.

This was Rob. This was me. This was *us*.

I tilted my head to deepen the contact, to shatter all those walls I'd erected against him. I pressed closer, wrapped my arms around his neck.

There could never be anyone else.

Only Rob.

We broke apart, maybe a minute, maybe an hour later. I'd lost all track of time in his arms.

He panted slightly as he rested his forehead against mine.

"Miss, I'm sorry."

"I know," I said. "I'm sorry too."

We stayed like that for a minute, huddled together in our perfect slice of the world.

But all things had to come to an end.

And this one, the first good one between Rob and I in what seemed like an eternity, was shattered by a text message.

How fitting.

37

*R*ob put down the phone and turned back to his wife, but he couldn't bear it. His eyes flicked away, around the kitchen that had mysteriously emptied when he'd started sucking his wife's face.

Fuck. He stood, thrust a hand through his hair, knew he was making it stand on end but not able to give a damn.

Not about his wife. He fucking loved having her in his arms. There was nothing better.

But he didn't usually do it in public.

He glanced back at her, ignoring the slice of hurt in her eyes, ignoring the cell phone on the table.

It wasn't the secret one. No, he'd given that one to the FBI when they'd showed up earlier that morning and told him they'd taken over the case. That they were the right big shots for the job, and all would be wrapped up in a nice little package soon. He just needed to sit at home and twiddle his thumbs like a good boy.

Never mind that *his* wife had been hurt. That she'd been targeted twice. Never mind that his blood was boiling and he wanted to cut the fuckers into little pieces for daring to harm a hair on her head.

He bit his tongue and forced his inner Neanderthal to stop raging and his brain to start working.

Rob had been a cop a long time. He understood the chain of command.

He knew this case was out of his league. The department didn't have the right resources, and clearly his cover had been blown.

But . . . Celeste was still in.

And she'd just texted begging for his help.

"Rob," Miss said, and he turned back to his wife. The beautiful woman he'd just finally started rebuilding bridges with, their peace tenuous at best.

"You have to go," she said.

His knees wobbled. Actually felt like Jell-O until he got his shit together and manned up.

"Miss, it's not—"

She pushed to her feet and took a step toward him, stopping with a wince and an annoyed breath. "Come here."

He closed the distance between them, pulling her off her feet, and sat in the chair, trapping her in his lap so she couldn't get away.

Not that she'd get far with her feet—

And damn, didn't that guilt feel great?

What had he gotten his family into?

"Hey," she said softly, touching his jaw and forcing his stare to hers. "I'm the one who's supposed to be good at guilt trips, not you."

He snorted. "Hilarious, Miss."

"I understand now, honey." She dropped her head to his shoulder and sighed. "I still think the way you went about everything was wrong. That we should have talked it out, but I made lots of mistakes too." Lifting her chin, she met his eyes again. The hurt wasn't completely gone, but it was tempered with regret and . . . with hope.

God, he sounded pathetic.

"But this"—she touched the cell on the table—"*this* is what you are. If someone needs help, you go. You *have* to. I know it, and I think you know it too."

"I—" Except the words wouldn't come. How could he leave his wife again after everything had happened?

How could he leave her for Celeste?

"It was never about—"

"Her." She shrugged. "I know that. Now." Melissa gave him the softest, sweetest smile. "It was about us."

He nodded, started to shift her back to her own chair.

"But," she said, and her voice took on an underlayment of steel he rarely heard. "You're not running off half-cocked. I know you can't bring the department back into this, not after handing off the case. So you need to talk to Justin's security team. You need to have a plan." She glared at him. "You have to do this as safely as possible."

"I will," he promised and felt his lips twitch up. "Half-cocked?"

Melissa sighed. "Oh my God. You're impossible."

"You love me."

She touched his chest, where his heart beat a rhythm that only she could create. "I do. Heaven help me, I do."

38

I watched my husband's back as he left the house after several hours of planning with Justin's security team, and although the view was familiar as of late, it wasn't accompanied by all the angst and hurt of the past months.

This time I was nervous for him and praying that he would be safe.

But I wasn't hurting.

For once I wasn't hurting.

My heart that was. I grimaced, tucked my crutches under my arms, and hobbled back to my bedroom. My feet were screaming for another pain pill, and my brain wanted sleep.

I knew I probably wouldn't get it, not with Rob out there, facing who knew what, backed by Justin's former military comrade's security team. I knew the men were capable, that they trained for just these matters. And I understood that Justin would never put his family's safety—or mine for that matter—at risk. But that didn't mean I would be able to relax until I saw with my own eyes Rob was all right.

So I put some boring documentary on Netflix and tried to ignore how slowly time was passing.

The kids would be up before I knew it and then I'd be suitably distracted, I thought as I broke a pain pill in half and took a sip of water to swallow it.

For now, binge-watching.

I must have dozed off during the documentary on Nixon's impeachment in the seventies—riveting content I know—but then I was suddenly wide-awake.

I sat up in bed, pressing the button on my phone to see what time it was.

Blinking against the bright screen, I saw it was just after five in the morning. Barely two hours after Rob had left, and yet, I couldn't shake the feeling that there had to be a reason I was awake.

I grabbed my crutches and aided by the pain pill—which was only making me feel *slightly* high and squidgy . . . which I didn't even know for sure was a word and was probably a sign that I was high as a kite—I made my way to the bedroom door.

It wasn't the most graceful journey, but I got the job done.

Then I carefully made my way down the stairs. But since I was drugged and could practically hear Rob's growling voice in my ear, I did it by sitting down and scooting on my tush the entire way.

No headers down the stairs for me, thank you very much!

I made my way to the fridge and started pulling out ingredients for a breakfast casserole. I was awake and might as well make the most of it. But just as I'd set the milk on the counter and was reaching for the carton of eggs, my new phone rang.

Loudly.

"Dang," I muttered, realizing that I hadn't programmed the settings on the new cell Danny had given me. I lurched for it, swiping my finger across the screen. "Hello?" I huffed, leaving my crutches for a moment and using the wall to make my way out the kitchen door and on to the back porch.

"Melissa!"

"Tammy!" I said. "Hi!" My voice was too bright, and I knew it.

So, apparently, did Tammy. "What's wrong?" she asked. "Why

are you out of breath? Oh, God. Did I interrupt something with that hubby of yours—"

"No!" I said quickly. "I hurt my feet is all."

"Your *feet*?" she said, incredulous. "As in both of them?"

"Yes." I waved a hand. "It's a long story. I'm fine. Anyway, I was trying to go outside so I could talk without waking the house."

I heard rustling, imagined her looking down at her phone to check the time. Then more rushing, and she was back. "Oh shoot, honey. I didn't realize it was so early out there. Sometimes I lose track of the time zone thing. I hope I didn't wake you."

I smiled. "It's okay. I was already awake."

"Cooking?" she asked.

"Of course."

"What recipe?"

I shrugged, silly that it was since she couldn't see it, then said, "I wasn't really going to follow a recipe. I was just going to make a breakfast casserole with bacon and potatoes and eggs."

She swallowed, and I could practically hear the drool through the airwaves. My talk of bacon and potatoes was making me hungry too. Especially when she asked, "Cheese?"

I chuckled. "Of course."

"Yum." Then her voice went stern. "I'll need pictures after you're done of course and"—she laughed—"maybe to come visit."

"You sound like Kelly now," I said.

"Aw. How is your sister?" Tammy asked.

"Pregnant," I said. "With twins."

"What?" Tammy shrieked a little. "Omg! Those babies are going to be adorable."

I sighed. "I know, right?"

"So right." She laughed again. "I feel like I'm jumping all over the place here, but we always seem to get off topic when we talk, like we're old friends just phoning for a chat."

"I feel the same," I told her.

"I'm glad. And doubly so because the network feels the same! They want to offer you a contract."

"What?" My voice was shrill. Happy. Shocked. But still shrill. "Are you serious?"

"Do croissants have butter?"

"Oh my God!" I slumped back against the wall. "I can't believe this. I—just—*oh*— This is amazing! Thank you, Tammy. Thank you so much."

"You did it on your own, honey. I'm just happy to be part of the process," she said. "I'll send the contract over. Take a look then have a lawyer review it. I'd still like to use the ranch to film if possible, but we can talk more logistics later. I'm sure you want to share the news with your family."

We said goodbye, and I leaned against the house for a moment, feeling almost numb.

Had that really happened?

Or was it the imagination of a drugged up brain?

I glanced down at my phone, saw that the incoming call was logged there, clear as the memory of the conversation with Tammy was imprinted in my mind.

The squee in my throat bubbled up, but I forced it down.

I was going to have a cooking show.

It was going to be amazing.

Already my brain was filled with recipes to try out, ingredients to drive into Denver for.

There was this awesome cheese store in the city, and I could make something with spinach and Gruyere or a dessert with green apples and white cheddar. Traditional, mid-west, but slightly more refined.

And Rob loved the Havarti from there. I could bake up some sourdough and then make fancy grilled cheese sandwiches with it. Bacon. Caramelized onion jam. Maybe some Swiss for tang.

I paused. I think I'd figured out what my drug-induced obsession word was this time around.

Cheese.

I was already thinking of the block of cheddar on the counter as I turned for the door.

But—

I rotated back around, trying to figure out what had pinged my brain, what had made my spine go ramrod stiff with alarm.

The sun was still behind the hills, the sky just the slightest hint of pink, readying for the day. The air was chilled, and the lawn appeared black.

So what was making the hairs on my nape stand on end?

And then I saw something that should be black and was decidedly not.

Light poured out of the open door to the barn.

39

I didn't stop to think. Just shoved my feet into a pair of my sister's boots that sat on a rack near the door, thankful that she wore a size larger than my own as my stitches protested the action.

But I pushed the pain aside because the barn door was wide open. The lights were blazing.

My sister had been raised better. She knew to close the door behind her, to flick off the lights.

My daughter, on the other hand, did not.

And Allie's words from the day before were suddenly blazing through my mind.

"*I want to ride, Mom!*"

"*I can do it myself.*"

"*I don't need Aunt Kelly.*"

Part of me hoped that I was wrong.

The rest of me knew I wasn't.

So I took off across the lawn, my commandeered boots hurting worse than a sugar burn and the hems of my pajamas getting soaked by the wet grass.

I wasn't entirely familiar with the horses and who should be in what stall. Hell, I didn't even know exactly how many Kel owned at the moment or how many were boarding.

I did know that there was a sign near the tack room with each horse's name and their stall number, and so I went there first.

Which is probably why I didn't notice the open stall doors at first.

At least not until I'd noted where Allie's favorite horse was supposed to be and then hustled down to number twelve.

"What the—" I muttered, seeing that the doors at four, six, eight, and ten were all pushed open. I checked twelve just to be sure. I could have read the board wrong. Maybe Kel had moved the horses somewhere else? Maybe—

Hell. Who was I kidding? My sister was never more thorough or organized than she was with her horses.

Still, I checked twelve.

Because that was where Allie had to be.

Twelve was empty.

My eyes slipped closed, and I took a breath. My stomach was crawling with panic that I was desperately trying to swallow down. I didn't even know if anything was wrong yet.

I spun around and felt the toe of Kel's boot catch on something.

I bent and a wave of frost shot down my spine.

Mr. Tails was on the floor of the stall.

I didn't have time to think of a cooking curse word substitute. I couldn't come up with anything except . . .

"Fuck me."

And my phone rang.

This time my fingers fumbled to answer it for a completely different reason than Tammy's call from just fifteen minutes earlier.

This time I knew if I answered it, everything was going to go to hell.

I just knew it.

Yet, what other choice did I have? I needed to pick up.

After swiping my finger across the screen, I lifted it to my ear. "Hello?"

"You're a bitch, you know that?"

My voice had disappeared. I blinked dumbly. Both because the insult had taken me by surprise and also because I felt faint prickles of familiarity at the voice. It was female. Cold. And filled with hate.

Had I heard it before?

"Answer me!" the woman screamed.

My throat unclenched. "I'm sorry?"

"Damn right you should be," she hissed. "Or you *will* be. If you don't do exactly what I tell you." A pause. "Say you fucking agree, you dumb slut."

I closed my eyes, forced my pulse to calm. It was pounding so loudly in my ears that I could barely hear the woman. "I'll do whatever you want."

"You'd better. If you want to see Rob again." Her laugh wasn't maniacal, but it was damn near close. "Or your precious Allie."

There it was.

The reason I'd run to the barn instead of staying inside the house. The reason my palms were sweaty and my hands shook.

Allie.

I clenched Mr. Tails in my fingers, feeling the material strain under my grip. But I couldn't loosen it because . . . Allie.

"If you want to see your daughter alive, you'll saddle a horse and ride straight out from the barn. You'll go over the hills and then follow the old cattle trail south. From there you'll receive another phone call."

"But there aren't any horses—"

This laugh was maniacal. "There is one horse left. And he's a mean sucker."

My gaze flashed down the corridor to the odd-numbered stalls, and I saw one door was indeed closed.

Three. I frowned, trying to remember which horse would be there—which, I got was a really stupid thing to consider when the animal was the means to my daughter's safety, but my brain was my brain, and it was rapidly trying to digest everything that had happened in the last twenty or so minutes.

And that was a dream coming true followed by a hell of a lot of fucked up.

So I probably shouldn't have been surprised when Theodore popped his head over the door.

"Oh. There he is now," the voice in my ear said. I'd nearly forgotten about the phone, but now I whipped around, half expecting to find the woman in the barn with me.

How else had she known that Theodore had appeared?

"Look up," the woman said.

I did.

"Now wave to the cameras," she sing-songed. "And know that if you do anything except saddle that horse and ride out, your daughter will pay the price. No phone calls. No texts. No running into the house for some more of those security guards." Her voice went chiding. "Rookie mistake, by the way, letting Rob pull off the exterior guards for his rescue mission. The company should have known better and sent more men to cover the holes."

"They're—" I bit off the rest of my words, mentally kicking myself for almost telling her what Rob had planned for the security.

More guards were coming. Actually, they would probably be there soon. Justin had said they would be at the ranch near daybreak.

She laughed and I realized I *really* didn't like the way she did that. It sounded like shards of icicles were piercing my eardrums, even through the call's airwaves. I didn't like how cold it felt, how unhinged and frenetic.

And my daughter was with this madwoman.

"Who are you?" I asked, despite myself.

Another cackle. "You'll find out soon enough. Now you'd better move. Your fifteen-minute timer begins now."

40

*S*ince I didn't have any pockets, I shoved the phone into Kel's boot then ran down the hall to the tack room.

I had only the smallest clue what I needed, having been in the room with my sister a time or two. I scoured my brain, desperately trying to remember what she'd put on Sweetheart for our trail ride with her and Allie.

Thank God everything was labeled.

There was a section that said Theodore and in it sat a saddle, a blanket, and one of those things with reins that fit between a horse's teeth. I started to pick up everything I could then froze, glancing up and searching the corners of the room.

Were there cameras in here? Could I risk a call?

No. The cameras out in the barn might have microphones. And if that woman heard me not following her instructions . . .

A text! I could—

But dammit, what if they were tracking my phone somehow? They'd gotten past the security team once. Who was to say they hadn't hacked the cell?

Shit. I had to do something. My eyes scoured the room, searching for a brilliant idea. I was running out of time, so I grabbed the only thing I thought was safe.

Snatching up a marker, I wrote on the whiteboard posted near Theodore's gear:

Hills. South on cattle road. Phone call. Woman. Has Allie.

Please let someone see it.

Then I picked up the equipment and sprinted out of the room.

Theodore was staring at me, and I wondered if he'd kill me when I tried to saddle him. This was the horse that had kicked Kelly in the stomach when she'd been pregnant with Abby.

My sister said it had been a freak accident. That he'd spooked during a lightning storm, that he'd been hurt himself and hadn't meant to hurt her. She said he was actually a misunderstood sweetheart.

I hoped she was right.

I shoved open the door and slipped inside the stall.

"Fuck," I muttered. I really hated horses, and I especially hated how big Theodore was.

I dropped everything to the stall floor, jumping when Theodore snorted and pawed the straw with his hoof, but forced myself to calmly pick up the blanket and reach to put it over his back.

He shied away, snorting again and bobbing his head in a way that I knew was not happy.

Allie was out there. I needed to hurry. I *had* to do this.

Dammit. *How* was I going to do this?

I needed to channel Kelly. WWKD. What would Kel do?

"Hey, sweetheart," I said, speaking in the same tone I'd heard my sister use before. "Did some people come in here and scare you?"

He huffed.

"I'm sorry. They're scaring me too. And I think they scared Allie—" My voice caught, and I swallowed, reaching with the blanket again. This time Theodore allowed me to drape it over his back. "I don't know where they've taken her, but they say I need to ride you out over the hills. Can you help me do that?"

He turned his head slightly, eyeing me as I lifted the saddle and set it atop the blanket. Luckily I was fairly tall for a woman; otherwise, I never would have reached.

"I'm not sure that I'm even putting this on correctly," I murmured. "You'll let me know if I hurt you, right? I don't want to hurt you, Theo."

He moved so fast that I didn't have time to react. All of a sudden his head was next to mine, and I stumbled, trying to move back. I knew he'd bitten Justin before. But he didn't try to bite me.

Instead he rested his head on my shoulder for the briefest of moments and blew air in my ear.

And I felt my eyes fill with tears.

"Thank you," I said, arms coming up to pat his neck. "Thank you, Theo."

I buckled the strap around his middle and reached for the reins. Theo let me slip them up and over his head. I didn't think I knotted them correctly, but it was a joke to think I had a chance in hell of controlling Theo anyway.

The saddle was on. There were reins.

Now I just needed to figure out how to get onto his back.

Kel or Justin had always given me a boost in the past, and I had no clue where the mounting block that Allie usually used was.

And I was running out of time.

I opened the stall door and started to lead Theo out of the barn.

He froze and my heart sank.

"Please, boy. I need to find—" The words stoppered up in my throat when he knelt, seeming to invite me to climb onto his back. I scrambled up, felt the saddle sway slightly as he straightened and barely managed to hold my seat.

But it would do. It *had* to.

"When we get out of this," I said, lightly tapping his sides with my heels. "I'm buying you a whole truckload of apples."

———

I BUMPED AGAINST THE SADDLE, squinting in the dim light as Theo trotted or cantered, or whatever speed wasn't quite a full gallop for the hills.

"You can go a little faster," I said. "I'll hold on tight."

He made a horsey noise that was either agreement or disbelief but picked up the pace.

The wind whipped in my face, yanking my hair around. It stung as it slapped against my cheeks and the corners of my eyes.

This was just not for me, I thought as a bug flew into my mouth.

Up and over the hill we went, and I tugged gently on the reins, slowing Theo as I looked for the trail. "South," I said, mentally going through the old adage Never Eat Shredded Wheat, "is to the right. There!"

I guided Theo to the start of the trail, and he began to walk down the path.

My phone rang in my boot, startling both me and Theo.

"I'm sorry," I said, trying to retrieve it without losing my seat. "Hello?" I answered once I'd finagled the cell free.

"That was sixteen minutes," she said.

My heart squeezed. "I'm sorry. I went as fast as I could—"

Her voice sounded positively gleeful. "Do you *want* me to hurt your daughter?"

"No!" I practically screamed. "Please. No. Don't. I'll do anything you want."

"I *wanted* you to be where you are one minute ago."

"I'm so sorry," I said. "How can I make it up to you?"

"You can shut the fuck up," she snapped then sighed, not saying anything for a long minute. I wanted to go on begging, pleading, but I didn't think it would be wise when she'd told me to can it, so I waited, heart pounding, throat tight.

"Ride on this path until I call you again." She hung up.

I blew out a breath. "You heard her, right Theo?"

He snorted, tossed his head, and trotted down the trail.

41

The gunshot should have made Theodore spook.

It certainly made me almost lose my grip on the saddle, but Theo seemed to feel my weight shifting and moved, helping me regain my balance.

"Good horse," I said, stroking his neck as I kept my eyes on the person who'd stepped onto the trail in front of us.

By my guess, we'd been riding for close to an hour. The sun was just peeking over the horizon and though the world was still filled with shadows, they were growing less ominous and more like the real-life objects they were—trees, bushes, tall grass.

But the person—the *woman*—who'd stopped us on the path didn't look less frightening in the gaining light.

The gun in her hand certainly didn't set my heart at ease.

"Get down," she said, and hers was the voice on the phone.

"Why are you doing this?"

Click.

I knew that sound. It was the faint metal-against-metal noise of a gun's safety being removed.

"I said *get down*." She pointed the pistol at Theodore. "Unless you want me to shoot your perch first."

I lifted my leg from the stirrup and practically dropped from the saddle. It wasn't graceful, and my feet weren't prepared for the sudden weight. I ended up on my ass in the dirt with throbbing soles, but I'd gotten down.

The woman bent at her waist and laughed.

It was just as disturbing in real life as it was over the phone.

Ignoring her, I pushed to my feet and carefully stood in front of Theo, blocking him as I purposely let go of the reins and tried to shove him back in the direction of the barn.

He wouldn't budge.

"Go," I said, shoving his shoulder. At least I could save him. Or maybe someone would see him and realize—

"Freeze."

"Where's my daughter?" I blurted because the woman suddenly looked very scary.

She ran up to me and pressed the gun to the center of my forehead. "You don't speak unless I tell you to. You don't move a fucking muscle until I tell you to. Do you understand, you stupid, *stupid* bitch?"

I nodded.

Theo's head popped over my shoulder, and he bared his teeth.

The woman shoved his head away. "Shut up, you dumb beast."

Theo's teeth flashed, and he moved with the quick serpent-like speed he'd displayed at the barn.

He gripped the woman's arm and bit down. Hard.

She screamed, dropping the gun, and blood gushed everywhere. It was bright red, a crimson color that made me gasp and glance up at her mouth.

Because that was crimson too.

The same fire engine red I'd found on Rob's collar.

And I knew. Suddenly, I knew.

"Celeste," I whispered. Her eyes flashed to mine as she staggered to her feet.

I stumbled back against the pure hatred in her gaze, tripping over something in the dirt. Glancing down, I saw the gun had fallen between us.

I didn't think. I just dove for it.

The metal was warm against my fingertips, so much warmer than Celeste's icy hands as she grappled with my wrist.

For a second, she almost managed to rip it from my grasp, but I had a sudden burst of strength because I knew that if she took the gun from me that I was going to die.

It was the only bargaining chip I had, and I needed to keep it.

I tucked my feet between us and kicked her hard in the stomach. She grunted and held tight, both hands gripping and twisting my wrist. I felt something snap underneath my skin, cried out as a burst of white-hot pain shot up my arm.

But I didn't let go.

Instead I shifted the gun to my uninjured hand, tore my throbbing wrist free of her grip, and dug my fingers into the bite on her forearm.

She screamed, lurched away.

And I didn't let go. I moved with her, climbing on top of her and screaming at the top of my lungs, "Where the fuck is my daughter?"

"Funny, I was wondering exactly the same thing," came a cool voice.

I didn't have a chance to turn around and confirm my suspicion. The words had barely processed and my brain started pinging with alarm as it tried to comprehend—

Crack.

There was a flash of pain as something collided with my skull and then everything went black.

onya Harrison. In the flesh.

Sonya Harrison. My mother.

Sonya Harrison, who I hadn't seen in so many years that she was almost a stranger.

Almost because even though her face had more lines and her hair was more gray, even though her skin had that thin papery quality that only came with age, her eyes were still the same.

They were my eyes.

"Mom?" I asked. Questions pounded the inside of my skull. Or maybe that was the headache from whatever I'd been hit with.

I tried to push to my feet but found I couldn't. My hands were bound behind my back, my ankles tied together. What the hell was going on?

"Where's Allie?" I asked, head spinning as I tried to search for my daughter. I was no longer on the trail. Instead I was inside a dark room, just able to see the outline of several windows and a door from the cracks of light shining in through their perimeters.

Brighter sunshine. So it was later than when I'd been on the trail. But how much later? How long had I been gone?

Someone snorted, and a light flicked on.

I blinked against the brightness, and when my eyes settled, I decided that I liked the room better dark.

"Where's my daughter?"

"As I said earlier," my mother replied drolly, "that was my question. Though I guess I should have said I was wondering where my *daughters* were." Her gaze slid to Celeste's and went disapproving. "You know Cal doesn't like to be kept waiting."

Celeste's face clouded. "I don't give a fuck what Cal wants." She turned to me, and I think I would have been terrified by the malice in her expression if I weren't still processing the *daughters* comment.

Did she have Kelly? What about the babies? If they hurt her—

Celeste lifted the gun, and I cringed back.

My movement didn't matter. She aimed. Shot.

I screamed as the bullet tore through the skin and muscle above my knee.

Sweat broke out on my forehead, tears streamed down my cheeks. My wrist and feet, which had both been throbbing before barely registered a peep as a burning pain consumed me.

"You idiot," my mother screamed. "We need her! If she dies, we won't have a way to get the money."

"Kelly," I murmured.

"That's right," Sonya said. "We need Kelly." Firm hands pressed on my thigh, and I screamed again as something was wrapped around my leg and yanked tight. "Hush now. Cal will be annoyed enough without you carrying on."

"Take this." A slap across my cheek had me opening my eyes to a glaring Celeste. She held a little baggie of white powder in front of my face.

I shook my head. Drugs were a no and besides that, how was I supposed to take it? My wrists were still bound.

"Take it!" she screamed, hands grabbing for my mouth, no doubt to force it down my throat.

I'd heard of drugs being laced with fentanyl, knew that it had killed people. Aside from the fact that I'd never taken an illegal substance before, I definitely wasn't going to willingly consume whatever white powder was in that bag.

I could barely handle a half of oxycodone. Who knew what a bag of drugs would do to me?

"Stop."

The voice this time was different. And male. And—

I struggled to not empty the contents of my stomach on the floor as my mother squealed, launched herself into the man's arms, and latched onto his mouth.

This must be my mom's new flavor of the month.

The man, Cal I assumed, tolerated my mother's attention for all of ten seconds before he roughly shoved her away.

He was tall, probably several inches over six feet and built. His skin was tanned, almost weathered, as though he'd seen many days on the back of a horse. He reminded me of the ranch hands Kel hired to help out with the horses.

"Enough," he said and wiped his sleeve across his mouth. "You can blow me later. We've got things to do."

"You can always just do *me*, Cally-bear," my mother said, blinking coquettishly up at him.

I threw up a little in my mouth. Really, it was all so gross.

"Stop with the nickname," he ground out. "It's Cal. And we need to move with this." His eyes flicked to mine. "This her?"

My mother nodded. "My oldest." A snicker. "Though not the prettiest." She glanced across the room, and my stare frantically followed hers. Had I missed something? Was Kel here?

But Sonya's eyes didn't stop on my sister.

Or at least not on one I recognized. They came to a rest on Celeste.

Daughters.

Kelly wasn't here.

Daughters.

"Holy shit," I muttered.

Celeste smirked. "She's kind of slow isn't she?"

"Not the prettiest. Not the smartest," my mother confirmed.

I studied Celeste, tried to find some similarity, because could it really be? And if it was true, *how* could it be?

But as I looked more closely, mentally erased the full face of makeup, the crimson lips and smoky eyes, I saw that there was indeed a resemblance between her and my mother.

She had Sonya's mouth, the angle of her jaw. Celeste had Kelly's cheekbones, the same color of hair.

Son of a sinking soufflé, *she* was my sister.

"This isn't really happening," I said. "This can't be happening. This—this isn't—I can't. I've—" My voice gave out, the words stifling. My heart was pounding, my skin was clammy, and whether from the shock of the news or the gunshot wound, I very nearly passed out.

"Hey." A gentle hand touched my cheek. Cal was staring at me. "Your other sister isn't here. Neither is your daughter. This was a ploy to get you, you understand?"

His face had somehow softened despite the hard lines etched into the skin around his eyes and mouth. This was a dangerous man. An evil man. I could feel with every fiber of my being that he wouldn't hesitate to kill me.

And yet his caress on my face was tender. His voice soft.

It was absolutely terrifying.

"Do you understand me?"

Allie was safe. Kelly was safe. That was all that really mattered.

I nodded.

"Good," he said. "Let's go." He swung me up into his arms.

———

I DECIDED I didn't like the trunks of cars.

I also decided that if I didn't get out of *this* trunk, I was probably going to die.

It was cramped, dark, and disgusting. Something was sticky

against my cheek and I didn't want to think about what kind of bodily fluids were currently inches from my mouth.

But I'd discovered that I could almost get my hands below my feet and around to the front. The trouble was they kept catching on the heels of Kel's boots. So I was trying to wriggle the boots off and get my hands around, but the cable tie around my ankles and the *flipping* gunshot wound in my leg meant that it was a lesson in agony by inches.

Finally, I felt one of the boots begin to slide free. Slowly, *slowly* it slipped off and I was able to pull my foot loose and use it to toe off the other. Without the boots on, the cable tie was loose and I—

"Come on," I muttered through gritted teeth as I tried to yank my unhurt leg free. "Yes! *Finally.*"

Now I just needed to get my arms around to the front.

Carefully, I bent my knees to my chest, my injured leg screaming at the movement. I had contorted myself into a pretzel many times over for a yoga class. This wasn't any different.

Plus, my pain in this moment didn't matter.

Not if I wanted to live.

I had just inched my bound wrists past my butt when the car hit a bump. I cried out in pain as I was bounced around the unpadded space, but the jarring movement did what I probably wouldn't have been able to do on my own.

It freed my arms.

Well, they were still tied together, but they were in front of my body, and that meant I could finally do something.

I crammed them into my boot and pulled out my phone.

It had been buzzing against my leg consistently for the last ten minutes, and I hoped to God that meant that somebody knew I was missing.

My bound hands were too wide to reach my cell, so I turned the boot upside down then spent a good thirty seconds chasing the phone around the trunk when the car took a sharp turn and it slid away from me.

But then it was in my hands, and I pressed the button to light up the home screen.

There were over one hundred missed calls and more texts than I could scroll through.

I ignored them all and called Rob.

"Miss?" he answered before the call completed its first ring.

"It's me," I said.

"Thank God." He sighed. "Are you okay? Where are you? The barn. The sign—"

I slid across the trunk as the car made another sharp turn, whimpering when I banged my leg against something sharp.

It was a screwdriver and I quickly stuffed it into the waistband of my underwear.

"Miss? What is it?"

The car started to slow, and I knew I was running out of time.

"Listen, okay?" I said. "Don't interrupt." I paused and when he didn't speak, I hurried to get out as much information as possible. "My mom is behind everything. Her new boyfriend is named Cal. I don't know if he's a drug dealer or what, but he's dangerous. And there were drugs in the room and Celeste is here. She's my—" The air caught in my lungs. "Well, you won't believe it, but she's my sister, and she said she had Allie. I went to the barn, saw Mr. Tails. I thought they had her." I dropped my chin to my chest, my voice broke. "It was stupid. I know that now because they have me, and they're probably going to—"

They were probably going to kill me. I was going to fight like hell to prevent that. But I didn't hold any false hope.

There weren't too many scenarios where I got out of this.

"Melissa," Rob said. "I'm going to find you."

"Of course you are." My words were filled with a confidence I didn't feel as the car pulled to a stop. "I love you," I said and hung up the phone.

Because I was afraid.

Because I wanted the last thing my husband heard me say not to be a scream of terror or pain, but a declaration.

Of love.

43

*R*ob heard the phone click and lost his fucking mind.

"Fuck!" He whirled and put his fist through the wall of the chief's office. It made a satisfying crunch as it pierced through the sheetrock. "Fuck!" He yelled again and probably would have made another hole if not for his phone ringing a second time.

"Melissa?" he answered, not looking at the caller ID.

"No," came a male voice. "This is Dr. Johnson. Sam. The vet."

Rob was blinking slowly, trying to settle his heart rate and listen to the fucking man who'd flirted with his wife.

He assumed there was a reason the jerkwad was calling and it had better be good.

It was.

"Is there a reason I just saw your wife get pulled out of the trunk of a car on the old McKinney property?"

Rob's heart skipped a beat. "What are you saying?"

"I'm at the Sinclair Ranch checking on some injured cattle. I just saw your wife being pulled from the trunk of a car on McKinney land. There's an old barn just off route seventeen. It's maybe two miles beyond the last marker."

For a second, Rob couldn't say anything. Then he got his shit together. He glanced at the chief who hadn't said a word about him punching holes in the office wall but nodded at him now.

"Whatever you need," he said.

Rob nodded back. "Okay. Can you call Justin and have his security team meet us at the Sinclair Ranch? We'll proceed to the McKinney property on foot from there."

"Done," Sam said and hung up.

Everything that Melissa had told him in her rapid-fire recitation flashed through his mind. Celeste was her sister. Sonya involved. Drugs. And—

"Wasn't the lead FBI investigator who took over the case named Cal?" he asked the chief.

———

ROB PARKED his police car behind the Sinclair barn as the chief, Hayden, and McMann—the only officers, *friends* he'd trust with his wife's life—tore into spaces beside him, kicking up dust and rocks. Danny and the security team had beaten them to the location and were working on a plan to infiltrate the McKinney property where Melissa was being held.

Danny came over as Rob got out of the car. "I'm sorry," he said, shaking Rob's hand. "We should have waited until the new team came in before we left."

"They were watching. They knew they had to pull us out to get to her. And if Celeste is in this like I think she might be . . ." Rob shook his head and took the camouflage jacket and hat Danny handed him, along with an earpiece.

They'd rolled up to where Celeste had supposedly been held, the location she'd texted earlier in supposed panic, only to find the warehouse had been abandoned for some time. They'd known immediately something was wrong, but it had been too late, and by the time they'd gotten ahold of the security at the house, Melissa had been long gone.

She'd been smart, though, and thanks to her sign in the tack room they'd trailed her to an old outbuilding on the property. But aside from a large amount of blood on the floor, there had been no sign of his wife.

"It's beyond inexcusable—"

Rob cut him off. There would be plenty of time for the blame game later. "They would have waited for any moment she was unprotected."

He and Danny both ignored the way Rob's voice wobbled on the last word.

Because the last damn thing a man wanted to do was leave his woman unprotected, and he'd done just exactly that.

"We've got eyes on her. She's alive, and we're ready to move in an instant." Danny pointed at the cell Rob held in his hand. "Have they made contact yet?"

Rob tried not to notice how Danny had seemed to deliberately avoid the *and well* portion of *alive and well*. "No contact yet."

But the words had barely emerged from his mouth when his phone rang.

And not the one in his hand.

It was the other one.

Celeste's phone. Which had been returned to the chief by the FBI's lead investigator.

Who was named Cal.

This whole thing stank more than a barrel of week-old fish.

"Hold on," Danny said when Rob pulled the cell from his pocket and went to answer it. He gestured quickly to one of the men who handed him a device that he plugged into Rob's phone. "Location set?" he asked.

The man—Rob thought his name was Anthony—nodded. "Set to Justin's place."

"Go ahead," Danny said to Rob. "But you're not here. You're at Justin's. Quiet everyone!" he shouted.

"Got it." Rob swiped and put the phone on speaker. "Hello?"

"Robbie!" Celeste chirped. "Have you seen your wife? Because I have when I put a bullet in her."

Rob opened his mouth, ready to threaten her within an inch of her life, but Danny squeezed his shoulder, giving him a hand signal to calm down.

"Where are you?" he asked instead.

She laughed. "That is classified information." A tsk, and Rob heard typing in the background. "Ah good. You're where you're supposed to be. And you'll stay at your brother-in-law's ranch until I give you some directions." Her voice went hard. "No investigating on your own, that's how you got your wife into trouble in the first place."

A boulder settled in his gut. "What do you want?"

"You." Celeste cackled. "Just kidding. I want some of your brother in law's money. Five million. Cash."

Cold slid down his spine. "Celeste. I can't—"

"Oh, you will, Robbie," Celeste said cheerfully. "You will. Twenties and untraceable. I'm assuming you can do that by . . . oh, let's say midnight." She sighed, the air crackling through the phone's speakers. "Or perhaps sooner if you don't want Melissa to lose too much blood."

"Celeste—"

But she'd already hung up.

44

I was cold and getting more chilled by the second. We were in another room—only this one was actually a retrofitted barn and had been brazenly lit from the moment we walked in. Part of the reason it was so bright was because of the sun pouring in through skylights overhead.

The other reason was the heat lamps.

One full wall was filled with marijuana plants using said heat lamps. Two others held shelves with blocks of paper-wrapped packages. I didn't know if they held drugs or money, but I suspected there were both.

Near the door was a rack of guns. Illegal ones, by the looks of them. Or at the very least they vastly overpowered Rob's small police-issued handgun.

I was on the floor in the corner, trying to appear insignificant and attempting to stay out of sight.

I'd had enough time to slip my phone into my underwear—on the opposite side of the screwdriver . . . hopefully they wouldn't both fall out and give me away—and cram part of my foot into the cable tie around my ankle before the trunk had flown open. I hadn't been able to get my hands behind me, but no one had seemed to notice that particular detail.

So, I sat in the corner and watched the sun go down beyond the skylights.

"Here."

I glanced up and saw Cal had extended a bag of pretzels in my direction. I took them in my lap. "Thanks," I murmured, but I didn't eat anything from the open bag, only reached my hands in until he turned away, and then stashed the bag behind me.

I wasn't eating or drinking anything from this place.

Leaning my head against the wall, I stared back up at the skylights. I was in a strange sort of euphoria. Nothing hurt any longer, and while I was cold, I couldn't seem to muster up the energy to care about it.

I wondered if I was going into shock and if Rob somehow managed to find me—maybe track my phone—if I was going to die anyway.

The tourniquet on my thigh meant that I wasn't gushing blood, but I did have a steady drip that kept the cotton of my pajama pants wet and sticky. Add in my feet and my wrist—now purple and swollen—and I hardly felt human.

Which was probably why I didn't scream when I saw the shadow peer through the window.

Some angel of death had come to take me away.

Or not, I thought and blinked up at a man I'd only seen once.

Danny. From the security company.

I squinted and leaned forward, but Danny shook his head, raised a finger to his lips, and disappeared from sight.

That cold lethargy disappeared, and despite half my brain deciding that I had imagined the whole thing, the rest of me got ready.

I was down a leg, one arm, and the bottoms of both feet. But my ankles weren't bound, and I had the screwdriver down my pants.

By the way, that was a terrible euphemism that nearly made me snort aloud.

Not that the room at large would have heard it because the

moment I thought it, the front doors blew open. My mother screamed, Celeste grabbed a gun off the rack and began firing through the wall. Cal picked up a pistol and crouched in front of me, eyes moving between the disturbance at the front and the back doors.

What neither of them saw or heard were the windows shattering and the men rappelling in through the ceiling.

I'd not have believed something could be so efficient or rapid if I hadn't witnessed it with my own eyes, but I did see it, and it was amazing.

One tackled Celeste from behind, ripping the gun out of her hands and using his size advantage to pin and then handcuff her wrists and ankles.

Not so nice, was it bi-otch? I thought before my attention was pulled to Cal and the two men who were working to subdue him.

Blows were exchanged nearly faster than I could track, and he seemed to just be getting the advantage of one of the men when Danny grabbed him from behind in a choke hold and took him to his knees.

Thirty seconds later, he matched Celeste and was cuffed hand and foot.

Danny turned to me. "Are you—?"

"Where is she?" Rob thundered, sprinting through the debris at the front of the house. Hayden trailed him, the police chief two steps behind.

I opened my mouth. "I'm—"

The arm around my throat and the gun pressed to my temple cut off my greeting.

"Stop right there," my mother said, and I felt the *click* against my skull as she turned off the gun's safety.

"Sonya," Rob began.

"Where's the fucking money?" my mother screamed, and when I jumped she pushed the barrel even harder against my skin. "Shut up," she hissed and asked again, "Where is the money?"

"Sonya," Rob said, taking a step toward us.

"Don't move a muscle, Robert," she spat. "You were always an interfering little shit, and this is no different. You couldn't take Celeste's warning with that dumb dog of yours. No, you *had* to keep pushing and because of you Cal missed his chance at a drop." The gun came off my head, pointed at Rob. "You cost us fifty million, you son of a bitch." The barrel returned to my temple, dug in violently. "And just when we'd had you set up to take the fall, you had to go to the FBI."

"Where your husband works," Rob said softly.

I hadn't even known my mother was married again. I'd lost track of the number of husbands, in all reality. But it would have been really helpful to know she'd had an FBI spouse named Cal before Rob and the chief had gone to seek the government's help.

"You should have gone to ATF," I muttered. Or any other organization besides the FBI.

Rob's mouth quirked at the corner. "I agree."

"Shut up!" my mother screamed and yanked me to my feet.

I cried out in pain and collapsed to the floor.

"Stop being such a baby. The drugs on those pretzels should have you flying by now."

Except I hadn't eaten the pretzels.

Except the screwdriver and my phone had fallen from my underwear.

"Get up!" She yanked at my hair, and I barely had time to grip the screwdriver in both hands and get my good leg under me before the gun was back at my temple.

"The money's not coming," I said, shifting my weight slightly as I rearranged the screwdriver.

"Miss," Rob warned

I shook my head, twisting my shoulders to look up at my mother.

"You're always looking for that easy payday," I told her. "But I can tell you this time that it's not coming."

"Hate to contradict you, Melissa," Danny said. He tossed a duffle bag on the ground. "But the payday is here."

"Open it," my mother ordered as I slowly shifted my head from the gun. She still had a handful of my hair, but there was nothing to be done about it.

Especially when I saw Danny hesitate and knew the bag was only a distraction.

One deep breath and I moved.

Using a technique Rob had taught me long ago, I rotated under my mother's arm and brought the screwdriver up hard.

My hair ripped and my scalp was on fire. The tip of the tool met resistance . . . then that resistance was gone.

The screwdriver slid home.

I screamed and let go, falling to the floor as the men ran forward and grabbed my mother.

But I knew before I saw the empty, unseeing eyes.

I knew she was gone. Forever.

45

"*H*ere we meet again, huh?" Haley, the nurse who'd cared for me on my previous hospital visit said.

I made a face. "Not that I don't like you, but . . ."

She grinned. "I think you're just trying to get out of that cooking class you promised."

I laughed. "Get out of and cooking are words that I've never uttered."

It had been three days since the incident at the old McKinney barn, just over seventy-two hours since—

I closed my eyes against the bile that seemed to rise every time I remembered the incident, and since I seemed to be remembering the events every minute of every day . . .

"How's the pain?" Haley asked.

I peeled back my lids, watching her as she probed the bandage just above my knee and checked those on the soles of my feet. "It's fine," I said. "Nothing is hurting too badly."

She touched the splint covering my right wrist, glanced up at my face until my gaze locked with hers. "I didn't mean the physical pain."

"Oh." My eyes filled. "I'm okay. I just—"

"Am reliving it every second of every day?" she asked.

"Well . . ." I tore my eyes away, stared up at the ceiling. "Yeah."

"Don't let it fester, okay?" she said. "Promise me you'll talk to someone about it."

I tilted my head so I could look at her again. "You sound like you speak from experience on that."

Pink lips pressed together, and her pale skin went a shade lighter, making the freckles on her nose and cheeks stand out in sharp relief. But she didn't shy away from the eye contact. Instead, she straightened her shoulders and nodded. "You'd be right." She fussed with her ponytail. "It was a long time ago, but time doesn't always make everything go away."

"I—" But my words were cut off by a knock on the door.

"Hey," Rob said, and my heart fluttered. Like it used to, like it was filled with butterflies.

"Hi," I said and couldn't find the words to say anything else. I just stupidly stared at him.

"I'll see you soon." Haley squeezed my shoulder. "Don't forget what I said."

"I won't."

Rob came into the room, plunking himself in the chair at my bedside. The chair he'd refused to leave from the moment I'd come out of surgery, until I'd forced him out of it that morning in order to go home and shower.

"How are the kids?" I asked.

"Anxious to see you again." They'd come yesterday when I finally felt like I wouldn't scare them.

I swallowed hard. After I'd stabbed my mother—*no, Sonya,* because she was no mother to me—the tourniquet around my leg had given way, and I'd lost a lot of blood really fast.

It had apparently been touch and go there for a while, Justin working on me in the back of a police car as Rob had rushed me to the hospital.

In some ways, I felt lucky that I'd passed out and hadn't been awake during those frantic moments.

I had enough nightmares to last me.

"Will you bring them after school?" I asked.

He smiled. "Only way I could get them to agree to go in the first place."

"They love school."

"They love you more."

I sniffed, felt my eyes well. "No fair. I'm supposed to be keeping fluids in, not losing more."

Rob's face sobered, and he went very, *very* still.

"What?" I asked.

His gaze dropped to the bed, and he picked up my uninjured hand, laced his fingers through it.

"I thought I'd lost you," he said softly.

"Justin wouldn't have let that happen," I said.

"Not then."

The serious tone of the words made my breath catch. "We almost lost each other, Rob."

He shook his head. "I—"

There was another knock at the door, interrupting his words, though I almost felt it was timely.

Because I had the feeling this conversation was one that Rob and I were going to need to have many times over.

"I'm sorry to interrupt," came a male voice.

"Sam!" I exclaimed.

The vet walked into the room, glanced at Rob and my inter-laced hands, and smiled. "I heard that you're going to be discharged tomorrow and wanted to talk to you about Rocco."

My stomach clenched. "Is he okay?"

Sam put a hand up. "Totally fine. He's been staying at my house because I wanted to make sure you guys were ready for him. Do you want me to keep him a few more days? Or to bring him over tomorrow?"

"Tomorrow," both Rob and I said.

Sam nodded. "Okay then. I'll just head back to the clinic—"

"A word?" Rob said.

"I don't—" I began, but Sam said, "Sure."

Rob stood, pressed a kiss to my lips. "I'll be right back. Outside," he said to Sam once he got closer.

"I—"

But they were gone, through the door, and I couldn't follow them.

"Ugh," I muttered and stared up at the television screen. It was on Tammy's food channel, a celebrity chef whipping up a meal for her closest friends. The sight of the lovely cranberry, apple, and brie-laced bread was almost enough for me to forget about the fact that my husband may be coming to blows in the hallway with our vet.

I tried to convince myself it would be fine. Though Rob had been stiff and quiet, he hadn't been angry.

Or at least I hadn't been able to feel his rage as though it was a tangible thing, like the last couple of times they'd interacted.

I forced my gaze to the TV, tried to think of how I'd modify the recipe, and just was really beginning to worry when Rob stepped back into the room.

"Is everything—?"

"Everything is fine, Miss," he said. "Sam and I just needed to come to terms with a few things."

I narrowed my eyes at him. "What things?"

One half of Rob's mouth curved. "He was the one who spotted you being pulled from the trunk of the car on McKinney land."

"What?" All thoughts of bread disappeared. "*How?*"

"Luck," he said. "Sam was seeing to some injured calves on the Sinclair Ranch. It wasn't a place anyone would normally be." His voice gentled. "But we're lucky he was."

I nodded and knew that someone had been looking out for me that day. Normally, I wasn't religious or spiritual or whatever, but I couldn't explain away the feeling that I'd been slightly more than lucky.

Sometimes things just worked out.

"So I was thanking him. For that. For Rocco." He sighed. "For looking out for you when I didn't."

"Rob—"

"Hey, speaking of lucky," he said, obviously changing the subject. I think Rob and I *both* needed to talk with someone. Apart and, perhaps, together. "I think you've got a friend in Theodore."

"What?" I said, suitably distracted and then promptly guilty because I hadn't given the horse a second thought. "Oh my God. How could I have forgotten him? Is he okay?"

Rob grinned. "Temperamental as ever. I guess he showed up back at the barn as Justin and the hands were rounding up the loose horses and created all sorts of trouble."

"What trouble?"

"Would only let Justin get him and then when he was back in his stall, kicking and ramming the door until Justin let him out. When he still wouldn't settle, Justin finally re-saddled him and decided to give Theo free reign." Rob chuckled. "It's crazy, really, Justin came up to the McKinney barn like an avenging cowboy, dust cloud, pounding hooves and all."

I held my breath, imagining the scene, and glad, really glad that Theo was okay. The fuzz bucket was growing on me.

"Justin said that once Theo heard the shots, he started galloping and wouldn't stop. It's like he knew something was wrong and that Justin was needed there."

"A bushel of apples," I said, feeling suddenly exhausted.

"What?" Rob asked.

"I owe him a whole lot of apples."

Rob squeezed my hand. "I think you made a new friend."

I closed my eyes. "He's not so bad."

"No," Rob said. "He's not."

 ix Weeks Later

"AND STIR THAT IN." I grinned at the camera when Haley shrieked. "Slowly, sweetie. *Slowly.*"

Haley sighed and grimaced when she glanced down at her splattered apron. "Great," she muttered. "And now I've embarrassed myself on national television."

Kel put her hand to her belly, her twin-sized baby bump now beyond obvious. "At least you didn't attempt to dip yourself into the pancake batter."

We were making brunch on a live stream, a new addition I'd added to the blog. It had actually been Tammy's idea, to get me more comfortable with the camera before we began filming in a couple of weeks.

And it was great, actually. All of my social media sites had jumped in traffic, and I even had my own YouTube channel.

A big part of that was the recipes.

The other portion, I figured, was the national news coverage that had come from Rob taking down an FBI drug ring and my kidnapping. Celeste and Cal were currently in federal custody awaiting trial, and while I still didn't understand why my sister seemed to hate me so much or had decided that she needed to take some sort of vengeance on Rob and me, I was coming to terms with the fact that I might never know.

"I hear pancake batter is good for the skin," I said.

"Who says that?" Kel groused, wiping at her shirt with a towel. "Stupid belly getting in the way," she muttered.

"*I* say that." I grabbed Haley's arm to show her the proper motion for whipping the cream.

Yes, I did it by hand. Yes, it gave me nicely toned arms.

The cameraman snorted and I snagged the small camera from his hands. "Okay, Rob," I said, grinning into the camera before turning it onto my husband. "Since you seem to have something to say, you can do it on film."

Justin laughed, and I rotated to face him. "Do I need to commandeer you too?" He was sitting behind a laptop, reading comments and questions to us that were posted during the stream.

"Nope." He raised his hands. "Unless it involves taste-testing bacon."

We all laughed, and I returned the camera to Rob who gave me a once over and raised a brow.

I sighed. I knew what that brow meant.

It was the signal we'd come up with over the last weeks. His sign to me that he thought I was overtired and needed to wrap things up.

I smiled and nodded and where I once would have ignored the gesture, I'd learned to appreciate the thoughtfulness.

He was trying to help me. He was worried.

And my leg *was* aching.

So I sped into action, finishing the pancakes, plating them up for the five of us alongside the whipped cream, bacon, and egg casserole that had been resting in the oven.

Rob didn't intervene, though I knew it was hard for him. Especially when I stumbled as I turned and my knee nearly gave out.

Now *that* would have been embarrassing.

The TV cook upending multiple plates on camera.

But I righted everything in time, got everyone sitting down and eating, and we ended the live stream.

After five weeks of therapy—I'd taken Haley's recommendation straight away—and three weeks of rehabbing my leg, Rob trusted me to know my own limits.

Things weren't perfect, but we were finding our way.

He set the camera to the side, swept me up in his arms, and deposited me on the couch in the next room. Thirty seconds later, he'd returned with two plates and fed us both.

He might trust me to know my limits, but he also wanted to take care of me.

And I was learning how to let him.

Haley sighed when Rob brought the two plates to the kitchen then lifted me in his arms again and carried me back to join the others, plunking me onto his lap in one of the wooden chairs around the old oak table. "I need a man."

I smiled up at my husband. "Yes," I said. "They're not so bad."

EPILOGUE

Haley

"JUST PLAY ALREADY," Haley muttered, fumbling with her phone. She'd stopped at an intersection on her way home from the hospital, and she just wanted to boy band love, okay?

Exhaustion tugged at her brain, her eyes burned, and her shoulders ached. She was also very close to tears.

She'd lost a patient that night.

It hadn't been her fault. It hadn't been anyone's fault. Sometimes those things just happened—accidents, everyone working frantically to pull someone back from the brink, a body failing—but that didn't make losing a patient any easier.

Her job was to save them.

Life was such a fragile thing. As a nurse, she knew that first-hand. But she'd also left her job at the busy county hospital in California and returned home to Darlington, Utah because she was tired of seeing people die every day.

Haley was damned good at compartmentalizing, but sometimes things weren't so easy to shove down.

Sometimes those fuckers kept popping back up.

Sometimes the cases hit too close to home—

A horn beeped behind her and she jumped. "Shit." Her phone still not cooperating, the poppy upbeat notes of her favorite boy bands remained silently trapped inside the technological device that never seemed to work correctly.

Even though it was brand spanking new.

Even though she'd gotten a complete tutorial from her brother-in-law, who had gone through all the troubleshooting with her.

Even though the freaking tech from the phone store had personally tested the Bluetooth by coming out to her car and showing her how it worked.

Technology. She repelled it.

Or rather, she was technology's kryptonite.

Two minutes around her, and she destroyed even the most powerful device.

"Yay me," she murmured, dropping the phone to her passenger's seat. Haley shouldn't be fussing with it anyway, not while she was driving, but—*a sigh*—she'd really wanted to escape for the rest of her drive.

Not to be.

Checking for traffic, she pulled carefully through the intersection. Darlington was a small town, and signals were few and far between, but the roads at this time of the night were dark . . . and she'd had a deer jump right in front of her car once before.

The car that had honked at her turned to follow her down the bumpy lane, headlights very bright in her rearview mirror, the front bumper just inside that bubble all drivers had.

This one triggered her slightly-too-close alert but not the this-fucker-better-back-off alarm.

Her lips curved.

So, she might have gotten used to the more aggressive drivers of Northern California.

The thought of her first months in San Francisco, of the busy roads, the huge buildings, the patient care that both challenged and devastated her, brought a smile to her face. For all the reasons she'd come home, Haley was still happy she'd left Utah.

Small town life was . . . well, small.

Or it had seemed that way before she'd left.

Now she saw how much her world had expanded by being . . . well, herself. Having *found* herself, as cliché as that sounded.

She'd left a little girl, never feeling like she could measure up, and had returned—

Still feeling like she would never live up to her expectations. *Ha.* That was life for a girl. But Haley had come back with the understanding that *she* was the one setting impossible standards. Progress, yes? And she was a work in progress.

Step one was realizing that not everything she did had to be perfect and exacting.

Which was all well and good for her Pinterest attempts—*cough* —fails.

It didn't work as well for her patients.

Hence the mental punch fest happening in her brain alongside the driving need for cheesy pop music to provide her with some escapism.

Had she done everything right? What had she missed? What could she have done differently? Would any of it had made any difference?

No.

No, it wouldn't have.

Tears stung her eyes, and she blinked them away.

If Haley hadn't blinked at that moment, things might not have turned out as they did.

But she *did* blink, right as two other things happened simultaneously.

Music exploded through her speakers—the Backstreet Boys singing about the way they wanted it—and a deer jumped into the road.

By the time her lids had flashed back open, the jar of pop-tastic noise accelerating the process to near inhuman speed, the flipping deer was directly in front of her bumper and *definitely* within her bubble.

Frankly, it was firmly in the she-was-gonna-plow-it-down-and-make-a-deer-pancake zone.

"Fuck!" She slammed on her brakes.

Tires screeched. She braced for impact and then . . .

The deer executed a leap that was fitting of a figure skater and jumped clear of her car.

Haley sighed in relief. For a single heartbeat.

Because that relief disappeared before the next.

Her body was propelled forward as the driver who had been —and here came that damned bubble analogy again—following her too closely before, plowed into her from behind.

And she didn't even have time to snort about the dirtiness of that particular innuendo before the seatbelt yanked tightly across her chest. Pain shot up her leg as her foot compressed more firmly on the brake pedal, but before she could focus too much on the sensation, her head smacked against the top of the steering wheel.

"Fucking bubbles," she slurred as everything went black.

—Collision at Roosevelt Ranch Now Available

ROOSEVELT RANCH SERIES

Disaster at Roosevelt Ranch

Heartbreak at Roosevelt Ranch

Collision at Roosevelt Ranch

Regret at Roosevelt Ranch

Desire at Roosevelt Ranch

Did you miss any of the other Roosevelt Ranch books? Check out excerpts from the series below or find the full series here: amazon.com/gp/product/B07Q8VRK9Y

———

DISASTER AT ROOSEVELT RANCH
Book One
(books2read.com/DARR)

I had never thought of a plus sign as a bad thing.

Of course, I'd never had one show up on a stick I'd peed on. Kudos to me, that changed today.

My knees wobbled, and the idiotic white piece of plastic rattled as I set it on the scarred Formica countertop.

Brown eyes—mine—stared back at me accusingly in the mirror. "You've done it now."

A baby.

My hand found my stomach. Still flat, still the same.

Even though so much had changed.

The bathroom door rattled as a fist slammed against the thin plank of wood. "Move it, Kel! Food's up and your tables are restless."

"Coming!" I called as I wrapped the test in a paper towel before shoving it deep into my purse.

I couldn't leave it here. Not where anyone—where *Henry*—might see it. He would get his back up, storm out to the ranch where he-who-must-not-be-named lived, and drag the no-good, low down piece of crap into town for a proper whooping.

And I might just want to let him.

With a sigh, I washed my hands and left the bathroom.

It was my own fault. I knew the type of man Rex was.

I'd fallen into his bed anyway.

"Regret never fails to burn like a mother," I muttered as I

swept into the kitchen, grabbed the plates from the pass, and started hustling toward my table.

"What was that?" Henry asked as he flipped a burger.

"Nothing." I hefted the tray filled with six plates and various food accessories—ketchup, extra dressing, and napkins—with practiced ease.

Oh, God. I was going to be huge and pregnant and . . . waiting tables.

Good luck to the customers, because I lacked the sincerity and cheerfulness that seemed to come naturally to most waitresses on a normal day. I could only imagine what was going to happen when my hormones raged.

Using my back, I pushed through the swinging door and promptly stumbled to a stop.

He was here. *Rex* was here.

Stupidly, my heart raced. He'd changed his mind. He'd—

The man's eyes flicked to mine, completely unrecognizing and indifferent. My momentary burst of hope disintegrated.

He was going to pretend not to know me? To not *recognize* me? The jerk! The rotten—

Except . . . there was something off about him. I squinted, trying to discern the change, but the tray was taking its toll on my arms. I tore my gaze away from Rex to practically hurl the dishes at my customers.

"Anything else?" I asked, and was thankful when there weren't any requests.

Two seconds later, I was in front of Rex.

Who wasn't *actually* Rex.

Oh, he was the right height and had the same square jaw and the same gorgeous, sun-kissed skin, but *this* man wasn't the one I'd slept with.

"Hi," he said, his green eyes warm. They were a brilliant emerald and just as inviting as they'd been in the picture I'd seen on Rex's desk. "Can I just sit anywhere?"

My nod was jerky. "I'll get you a menu."

Fingers brushed my arm—calloused fingers that felt both familiar and different.

"You okay?"

I forced a smile, my stomach churning. This could *not* be happening. "Just perfect—"

And that was the moment I puked all over Rex's twin's shoes.

—Get your copy books2read.com/DARR.

———

COLLISION AT ROOSEVELT RANCH
Book Three
(books2read.com/CARR)

Haley

"Just play already," Haley muttered, fumbling with her phone. She'd stopped at an intersection on her way home from the hospital, and she just wanted to boy band love, okay?

Exhaustion tugged at her brain, her eyes burned, and her shoulders ached. She was also very close to tears.

She'd lost a patient that night.

It hadn't been her fault. It hadn't been anyone's fault. Sometimes those things just happened—accidents, everyone working frantically to pull someone back from the brink, a body failing—but that didn't make losing a patient any easier.

Her job was to save them.

Life was such a fragile thing. As a nurse, she knew that firsthand. But she'd also left her job at the busy county hospital in California and returned home to Darlington, Utah because she was tired of seeing people die every day.

Haley was damned good at compartmentalizing, but sometimes things weren't so easy to shove down.

Sometimes those fuckers kept popping back up.

Sometimes the cases hit too close to home—

A horn beeped behind her and she jumped. "Shit." Her phone still not cooperating, the poppy upbeat notes of her favorite boy bands remained silently trapped inside the technological device that never seemed to work correctly.

Even though it was brand spanking new.

Even though she'd gotten a complete tutorial from her brother-in-law, who had gone through all the troubleshooting with her.

Even though the freaking tech from the phone store had personally tested the Bluetooth by coming out to her car and showing her how it worked.

Technology. She repelled it.

Or rather, she was technology's kryptonite.

Two minutes around her, and she destroyed even the most powerful device.

"Yay me," she murmured, dropping the phone to her passenger's seat. Haley shouldn't be fussing with it anyway, not while she was driving, but—*a sigh*—she'd really wanted to escape for the rest of her drive.

Not to be.

Checking for traffic, she pulled carefully through the intersection. Darlington was a small town, and signals were few and far between, but the roads at this time of the night were dark . . . and she'd had a deer jump right in front of her car once before.

The car that had honked at her turned to follow her down the bumpy lane, headlights very bright in her rearview mirror, the front bumper just inside that bubble all drivers had.

This one triggered her slightly-too-close alert but not the this-fucker-better-back-off alarm.

Her lips curved.

So, she might have gotten used to the more aggressive drivers of Northern California.

The thought of her first months in San Francisco, of the busy roads, the huge buildings, the patient care that both challenged and devastated her, brought a smile to her face. For all the reasons she'd come home, Haley was still happy she'd left Utah.

Small town life was . . . well, small.

Or it had seemed that way before she'd left.

Now she saw how much her world had expanded by being . . . well, herself. Having *found* herself, as cliché as that sounded.

She'd left a little girl, never feeling like she could measure up, and had returned—

Still feeling like she would never live up to her expectations. *Ha.* That was life for a girl. But Haley had come back with the understanding that *she* was the one setting impossible standards. Progress, yes? And she was a work in progress.

Step one was realizing that not everything she did had to be perfect and exacting.

Which was all well and good for her Pinterest attempts—*cough* —fails.

It didn't work as well for her patients.

Hence the mental punch fest happening in her brain alongside the driving need for cheesy pop music to provide her with some escapism.

Had she done everything right? What had she missed? What could she have done differently? Would any of it had made any difference?

No.

No, it wouldn't have.

Tears stung her eyes, and she blinked them away.

If Haley hadn't blinked at that moment, things might not have turned out as they did.

But she *did* blink, right as two other things happened simultaneously.

Music exploded through her speakers—the Backstreet Boys singing about the way they wanted it—and a deer jumped into the road.

By the time her lids had flashed back open, the jar of pop-tastic noise accelerating the process to near inhuman speed, the flipping deer was directly in front of her bumper and *definitely* within her bubble.

Frankly, it was firmly in the she-was-gonna-plow-it-down-and-make-a-deer-pancake zone.

"Fuck!" She slammed on her brakes.

Tires screeched. She braced for impact and then . . .

The deer executed a leap that was fitting of a figure skater and jumped clear of her car.

Haley sighed in relief. For a single heartbeat.

Because that relief disappeared before the next.

Her body was propelled forward as the driver who had been —and here came that damned bubble analogy again—following her too closely before, plowed into her from behind.

And she didn't even have time to snort about the dirtiness of that particular innuendo before the seatbelt yanked tightly across her chest. Pain shot up her leg as her foot compressed more firmly on the brake pedal, but before she could focus too much on the sensation, her head smacked against the top of the steering wheel.

"Fucking bubbles," she slurred as everything went black.

—Get your copy at books2read.com/CARR

REGRET AT ROOSEVELT RANCH
Book Four
(books2read.com/RARR)

Henry

Henry wiped down the final table. He was beyond ready to go home and crash after a busy Sunday evening cooking at the diner.

He'd already flicked off the neon "Open" sign and dimmed the lights. The kitchen had been scrubbed and reset for the next morning's breakfast rush, and he'd sent Tilly off about an hour earlier—she'd had a date, and Henry didn't mind sweeping up or stocking the tables with all the necessities for the next day.

Paper napkins, ketchup, salt and pepper, sugar. They weren't what had been on the tables in the Michelin-starred restaurant he'd cooked at while living in New York five years before, but they were his childhood.

His way of feeling close to his dad.

God, he missed his dad.

The bell hanging on the front door rang, and he mentally cursed at having forgotten to lock it.

Beginner mistake.

He'd worked half his childhood in the diner, had closed it down more times than he could count.

And somehow, he'd forgotten to lock the front door.

Hopeless.

"I'm sorry, we're closed," he said, deliberately not looking as he reached to straighten a salt shaker that was slightly askew.

"So, this is your place, is it?" The softly accented voice made him freeze.

Italy. Warm Tuscan sunlight, softly rolling hills through wine country. Cheese and pasta and pizza and . . . *her.*

He accidentally knocked the shaker to the floor. It didn't break because this was a family place and they'd learned long ago that plastic was safer with the kiddos, but Henry watched in slow horror as the lid popped off and salt spread out on the tile floor.

Though his horror didn't come from the spilled salt.

No. It came from the fact that she was there.

He turned. Saw for sure he hadn't been mistaken.

She was there.

Isabella Mariano was in Darlington, Utah. Inside his restaurant.

"*Buona notte*, Henry."

He'd last seen her as she'd gotten on a plane heading the opposite direction of where he'd needed her, flying away when he'd asked her to stay, bolting while his heart had been left to shatter.

"Isabella," he said coldly.

If she noticed his tone, she didn't comment on it.

Then again, she was good at that.

"What are you doing here?" he prompted when she didn't say anything further.

She swept over to him, heels clicking on the tile floor, more beautiful than ever. Her brown hair fell in perfect waves, her killer body was clad in sleek designer clothes, and a diamond ring on her left ring finger sparkled in the dim light.

Diamond ring.

On her left hand.

He processed that, but her words still hit him like a two-by-four to the temple.

"I want you to cater my wedding."

—Get your copy at books2read.com/RARR

DESIRE AT ROOSEVELT RANCH
Book Five
(books2read.com/DesireARR)

Rex

He drove down the dark road, trying to figure out why he was still in Darlington, Utah almost two months after he'd deposited Bella back with her one true love, Henry.

Barf.

Love was for idiots.

Or pussies.

Or people who were insanely, sickeningly happy.

Ugh.

Rex was jealous. He knew it. He embraced it.

But that didn't change the fact he wasn't the kind of person who fell in love. Or rather, he didn't *allow* himself to fall in love. He'd seen the way his father had loved his mother—a touching Hollywood scene if there ever was one, filled with so much devotion and affection that when she'd died, he'd changed.

Part of him had died, too.

And so Rex and Justin had lost *both* parents.

That was the troubling part of so-called happily ever afters.

They never lasted.

Rex sighed because the real casualties in those failed or aborted happy endings were the kids. *They* suffered. *They* lost it all. *They*—

"Fuck!" he said and swerved, almost clipping the car pulled barely on the shoulder.

No hazard lights flashing. No flares. Nothing but a dark shape silhouetted against the moonlight. Were they trying to get themselves killed?

He slowed and turned around, heading back to the parked car.

His tirade about responsibility was on the tip of his tongue and—*ha*—if anyone even knew that *he'd* thought the word responsibility, they would have keeled over and dropped dead.

Responsibility and Rex Roosevelt did not belong in the same sentence.

He was the screw-up.

He was the bad guy.

He was pulling over behind the car.

Rex parked behind them and turned on his hazard lights before getting out. He'd extended a hand to knock when he saw the woman inside. Spot-lit by his car's headlights, she looked like an angel with pale blonde hair and delicate features.

Or at least from the glimpse he caught, they *seemed* delicate.

He only caught hints of a pert nose, plump lips, and a petite chin because she was spending a lot of time banging her face against the steering wheel.

Rex hesitated and almost turned away, leaving her to whatever sort of mental breakdown she was determined to have, but just as he'd taken a step back toward his car, his conscience pinged.

The annoying bastard had been all too busy lately.

He sighed but knew he couldn't leave her, and so he blew out a breath, raised his hand, and knocked on the window.

The woman inside jumped.

Her gaze shot to his for one long moment before her eyes slid closed, head dropping down to the steering wheel.

But Rex barely noticed.

Because one look from *her,* and he'd felt like he'd been struck over the head by a two-by-four.

Or maybe hit in the ass by Cupid's arrow.

She was . . . different . . . wonderful . . .

And he wanted her.

—Desire at Roosevelt Ranch coming November 17th

ALSO BY ELISE FABER

(see a full listing and descriptions at www.elisefaber.com)

Roosevelt Ranch Series (all stand alone)

Disaster at Roosevelt Ranch

Heartbreak at Roosevelt Ranch

Collision at Roosevelt Ranch

Regret at Roosevelt Ranch

Desire at Roosevelt Ranch (Nov 17, 2019)

Billionaire's Club (all stand alone)

Bad Night Stand

Bad Breakup

Bad Husband

Bad Hookup

Bad Divorce

Bad Fiancé

Bad Boyfriend (Jan 2020)

Gold Hockey (all stand alone)

Blocked

Backhand

Boarding

Benched

Breakaway

Breakout (Dec 2019)

Life Sucks Series (all stand alone)

Train Wreck

Phoenix Series (read in order)

Phoenix Rising

Dark Phoenix

Phoenix Freed

Phoenix: LexTal Chronicles (rereleasing soon, stand alone, Phoenix world)

From Ashes

KTS Series

Fire and Ice (Hurt Anthology, stand alone)

ACKNOWLEDGMENTS

This is the point in every book where I freak out. Because I know I'm going to forget someone. Sometimes writing feels a very solitary career, day after day of just me and my computer, Sally (yes, she has a name. Yes, that's crazily anthropomorphic, but I'm mean and that means my brain works in mysterious ways). But I digress.

There are so many people that keep me sane, allow me to bounce covers and plot ideas and book titles off of that it would be impossible to name them all (though K.C. you especially rock!). This is the point that I remember I'm not a solitary creature and that a ton of people help me morph my scattered ideas into a real, working book.

Thank you to my editors, Adriel, Kay, and Christine. You never fail to jump in and save me when time gets tight or when I have a freak out about a hyphen or when I change a character's age or eye color (looking at you, Adriel). And thank you to my fan group, The Fabinators, who have been with me for so long and show so much support! You're awesome.

Okay, I've blabbed enough, but before I go, I want to give an especially big thanks to Sara. You may no longer be my assistant (tears!!) and I'm so sad to lose you to full time employment, but

I'm looking forward to what your future holds and know that you deserve all the happiness and good things in the world. I love you!

Oh! And see I almost forgot someone! YOU. Because I couldn't do it without you guys! Thank you for continuing to support me and my books. I love you guys!! I also love keeping in touch, so go ahead and join my fan group. It's fun, I promise!! (http://www.facebook.com/groups/fabinators) Or feel free to email me (elise-faberauthor@gmail.com), or reach out to me via my website (www.elisefaber.com).

-XOXO, E

ABOUT THE AUTHOR

USA Today bestselling author, Elise Faber, loves chocolate, Star Wars, Harry Potter, and hockey (the order depending on the day and how well her team -- the Sharks! -- are playing). She and her husband also play as much hockey as they can squeeze into their schedules, so much so that their typical date night is spent on the ice. Elise is the mom to two exuberant boys and lives in Northern California. Connect with her in her Facebook group, the Fabinators or find more information about her books at www.elise-faber.com.

    facebook.com/elisefaberauthor

    amazon.com/author/elisefaber

    bookbub.com/profile/elise-faber

    instagram.com/elisefaber

    goodreads.com/elisefaber

    pinterest.com/elisefaberwrite

Made in the USA
Monee, IL
30 September 2021